"I owe you an explanation, and this isn't something I can rattle off in a few quick sentences.

"It's complicated, and it's important that you understand. Things can get serious when you're working for Lorenzo. Tonight, you saw how bad it can get."

"Three murders. It doesn't get much worse."

"Last night, I promised that I'd protect you. That's what I mean to do."

Angie turned so she could see what was going on behind her. In a quiet voice, she said, "What if I don't want your protection?"

"I'm not trying to insult you or say that you're weak. But you're new in town and really don't know what you've gotten yourself into."

"You think I should stay safe, keep my head down, do my job and not make waves. I should be a good girl, an obedient girl. Take no risks. Then I won't get hurt."

"I'd never try to tell you not to make waves. That's not your nature. Angie, you're a tsunami."

"You bet I am."

USA TODAY **Bestselling Author**

CASSIE MILES

To Matt and Lauren, fantastic cooks. And, as always, to Rick.

Recycling programs for this product may not exist in your area.

ISBN-13: 978-1-335-48923-4

Find Me

This edition published by arrangement with Harlequin Books S.A.

For questions and comments about the quality of this book, please contact us at CustomerService@Harlequin.com.

Harlequin Enterprises ULC
22 Adelaide St. West, 40th Floor
Toronto, Ontario M5H 4E3, Canada
www.Harlequin.com

Printed in U.S.A.

Cassie Miles, a *USA TODAY* bestselling author, lived in Colorado for many years and has now moved to Oregon. Her home is an hour from the rugged Pacific Ocean and an hour from the Cascade Mountains—the best of both worlds—not to mention the incredible restaurants in Portland and award-winning wineries in the Willamette Valley. She's looking forward to exploring the Pacific Northwest and finding mysterious new settings for Harlequin Intrigue romances.

Books by Cassie Miles

Harlequin Intrigue

Mountain Retreat
Colorado Wildfire
Mountain Bodyguard
Mountain Shelter
Mountain Blizzard
Frozen Memories
The Girl Who Wouldn't Stay Dead
The Girl Who Couldn't Forget
The Final Secret
Witness on the Run
Cold Case Colorado
Find Me

Visit the Author Profile page at Harlequin.com.

CAST OF CHARACTERS

Isabel (Angie) D'Angelo—Undercover FBI agent whose disguise is platinum-blond hair and pink rhinestones.

Julian Parisi—Also known as Professor, he is the general manager of Nick's, a gentlemen's club in the Colorado Mountains.

Nick Lorenzo—The big boss of a Denver-based crime organization who plans to get into human trafficking.

Valentino—Known as the Baker, he owns several shops called Valentino's Bakery and Wedding Cakes.

Nolan Zapata—Chief number cruncher for the Lorenzo crime organization.

Calamity Jane—Burlesque dancer who performs with whips.

Marigold—Angie's childhood friend.

Chapter One

The dark blue delivery van chugged across the motel lot and parked beside her Toyota hatchback sedan. Though the logo on the side of the van—Valentino's Bakery and Wedding Cakes—seemed innocent enough, Isabel D'Angelo suspected trouble. Today, she was supposed to meet with a couple of the top honchos from Denver's most extensive crime organization to talk about a job, but they hadn't contacted her. Not a text or an email or a simple phone call. Why not? Had the deal gone sideways? Did they find out that she was undercover for the FBI?

Angie shook off her doubts. If she hoped to convince anybody that she was a math whiz with a special talent for money laundering, she had to totally believe her own cover story. More than confidence, she needed swagger, and she had to get it right the first time. Posing as a criminal wasn't really a far stretch for her. Though she'd graduated number one in her class at Quantico, she'd been a delinquent teenager. Her natural talent for deception was one of the main reasons she'd survived in the foster system. Lying came easy.

Peering through the slit between the cheap motel curtains and the cold window frame, she watched two guys—one in a suit, the other in a black leather jacket—leave the van and approach her room. A gust of October wind flipped back the older man's suit coat, and she saw a holster. He was armed. Nervous tension heightened her senses as she slipped into a leather jacket of her own—pink and studded, of course. A long time ago, she'd learned to use style, sparkle and flash as distractions. She tightened her long, sleek, white-blond ponytail and applied a fresh coat of fiery red lipstick.

She whipped open the motel room door and confronted the men. "You're late."

"The boss didn't tell you when we'd be here," said the man in a gray business suit with an open collar blue shirt. He was nondescript, bland and about five feet nine inches tall, which matched her height without shoes. In her specially designed platform combat boots, she was close to six feet tall.

"It's after four," she said, as if criminals kept regular business hours.

"Let's go, Angie."

"I didn't catch your name."

"Carlos."

"Nice to meet you, Carlos." She closed the door to her motel room and went forward, brushing past the two men. "I'll take my car and follow you."

"You ride with us."

From the corner of her eye, she saw the guy in the black leather jacket reach toward her in an attempt to grab her upper arm. *Did this dope really think she'd allow him to manhandle her?* Angie's self-defense moves were practiced and precise. She yanked his thick wrist behind his back and twisted hard. After a chop to the back of his leg, he dropped to a knee. While keeping pressure on his wrist, she flipped open the monogrammed switchblade she'd taken from a special pocket in her skinny jeans and waved the razor-sharp edge in front of his face.

Though her pulse was racing like a jackrabbit facing a rattlesnake, she stifled any sign of nerves. It was important to establish her identity as a dangerous person, even though she was cute, skinny and female. "Your name?"

"Murph." His ID sounded like the bark of a mumbling mutt...*murph, murph, murph.*

She released him and took a step back in case he decided to lash out. "Here's the deal, gentlemen. I don't want trouble. If it's important that I ride with you, fine. Just ask nicely."

"Sure," Carlos said. A smirk twisted his thin lips, and she had the impression he'd enjoyed her confrontation with Murph. "Please, Miss Angie, would you join us in the van?"

"Don't mind if I do."

She climbed into the rear. This windowless area wasn't meant for passengers. A lingering scent of vanilla and sugar, plus a couple of white pastry boxes tied with string indicated that the vehicle actually was used to transport baked goods. She perched on the edge of a bench seat on the wall. Murph—still cradling his wrist and acting as though she'd hurt him—slid behind the steering wheel.

In the passenger seat, Carlos turned so he could see her. "I have one more request. Until we know you better, the boss insists that you wear this."

A black hood dangled from his forefinger, and she stared at it in disgust. "Why?"

"This isn't negotiable." His smirk deepened. "Would you, pretty please?"

She snatched the hood from his hand. "I'll do it, but this is a waste. I'm new to Denver and don't know my way around. I couldn't tell you where we are or where we're going."

The lie rolled easily from the tip of her tongue. When she was fifteen, she'd spent six months living on the streets of this city after she ran away from her foster home in Utah. That was eleven years ago, but there were parts of this town she'd never forget. Since yesterday, she'd been studying maps and computer images of Denver and the surrounding area. Knowing various locations and resources could be vital to her survival.

Riding in the back of the bouncy van with the black hood over her head provided an opportunity to plan and to focus. Her goal today was to get hired by the sprawling crime business that had taken root in Denver during the post-WWII population boom. Her entry point would be through their gambling and money laundering operation, but her endgame involved gathering enough information to destroy a brand-new start-up project that might turn into the biggest human trafficking ring west of the Mississippi.

Unlike her other undercover assignments, mostly in California, she had a personal stake in bringing down the patriarch, Nicolas Lorenzo. During her stint as a runaway in Denver, she'd lost a friend who had been swept up by criminals involved in the sex trade and never seen again. Angie didn't have many friends, and she'd loved Marigold. She'd sworn that someday she'd get even.

Someday was almost here.

Though she was unable to see, she could tell a few things about their route from shifts in direction and changes in the light that filtered through the hood. They'd gone southwest, hadn't taken a highway. She really hoped they weren't headed into the mountains. Angie wasn't a fan of the unmapped hills and forests. After a few bumps and a downward turn, she guessed that they were driving down a ramp into an underground parking structure.

After they parked, Carlos pulled open the door to the van and took her hand to help her climb out. "I need for you to keep that hood in place until I tell you to take it off."

"It's hard to walk."

"Don't worry. I won't let you bump into the wall."

Without vision, she was thrown off-balance. Instead of facing Lorenzo with her head held high, she'd be forced to approach tentatively, clinging to Carlos like an invalid. No doubt that had been their plan: make her feel helpless so she'd be more cooperative.

Carlos guided her into an elevator. When they emerged, she shuffled her feet and felt carpeting on the soles of her boots. Carlos guided her through a door, taking care so she didn't run into anything. He seated her in a padded chair before he whipped off the hood.

Angie blinked at the late afternoon light pouring through a wall of windows into a conference room. As soon as she could focus, she found herself staring into the most crystal-clear blue eyes she'd ever encountered. Deep set and framed by long, dark lashes, those piercing eyes dominated a square-jawed face with high cheekbones. His scrutiny disrupted her composure more than the van ride or the black hood. He seemed to be assessing her, taking her measure and making a judgment.

Dragging her gaze away from him, she checked out the other two men seated at a round table. To her disappointment, neither was Nicolas Lorenzo. Carlos took the empty chair to her left and dismissed his partner. As soon as the door closed, Carlos regaled the others with the story of how she'd bested Murph in the motel parking lot.

While he talked, she watched their expressions. The man with the incredible eyes barely reacted. Who was he? The other two were familiar from her research into the Lorenzo family, but she knew nothing about this guy with the rugged features and thick, curly, dark blond hair.

He continued to watch her, and she endeavored to match his cool resolve. She busied her hands to keep her fingers from trembling. From a pocket of her pink jacket, she took out a lipstick. There was a mirror on the side of the tube, and she used it to apply a fresh coat of bright red. When she pursed her full lips and smoothed her platinum hair, she saw that the men had stopped talking to watch her. She had their attention.

"Gentlemen, I'm Isabel D'Angelo. I go by Angie. Some people call me a genius when it comes to numbers. Hire me and I guarantee to boost your profits."

"How much is this going to cost?" asked an extra-large man who barely fit into his chair.

"Not a dime," she said. "I take a commission from a percentage of the profits."

"You come with high recommendations, if you know what I mean," said the man opposite her.

"I think I do."

"Our associates in San Francisco like you. I'm Nolan Zapata. This big ape sitting next to me is Valentino the Baker. And that's Julian Parisi, otherwise known as the Professor."

She could have sworn that Julian's firm handshake ignited an electric spark that sizzled up her arm and elevated her core temperature by several degrees. All the while, he never broke eye contact. "We have a mutual friend," he said, "Manny Harris."

"Not a friend of mine," she quickly responded, tossing out another lie. Harris was with DEA and had successfully infiltrated a drug cartel before recently being reassigned. Why would Julian mention him? Was he testing her? She tried to pull her hand from his grasp but he didn't let go.

"Where did you learn your math skills?" he asked.

"MIT." She'd been telling this lie for so long that she almost believed it herself. "I had an uncle in Reno who showed me how to put all that academic data to use in gambling."

"Handy."

"Why do they call you Professor?"

"For one thing, I got brains." He reached into the pocket of his dark blue blazer, took out a pair of black frame glasses and perched them onto his nose. "When I'm wearing these, people tell me that I look like I should be standing in front of a classroom."

Angie never had a teacher who had blue eyes that could stare into her soul. If she had, she might have been more motivated to stay in high school. "I'll call you Julian."

"Now that we're all friends," Zapata said, "I want to make you an offer, Angie. We can use somebody with your skills, but you've got to prove yourself. I'll give you one week to reorganize our OTB operation."

"Horses?"

"That's what off-track betting means."

Her dislike for the massive beasts was pure truth. Animals were as unpredictable as children and almost as annoying. "I'd rather handle sports betting, even soccer."

"It's not your choice, honey." Zapata gave her a dismissive nod. "I'll check in with you, and I will expect higher profit after next weekend."

"It's already Thursday," she pointed out. "I can't make big changes in such a short time. Give me a month."

"Ten days," He emphasized the finality by whacking

the flat of his hand on the table. "I hear you're a smart girl. You'll figure it out."

There was an implied threat behind his words. The Lorenzo organization wasn't about to open their books to just anybody. "You won't be disappointed."

"I need to take your cell phone," Julian said. "Security reasons. Don't worry, I'll give it back."

She'd expected as much. All her contact numbers had already been cleared and sanitized. She took the red-gold phone from her jacket pocket and placed it on the table. "I want it back as soon as possible."

"Your password?"

With her manicured and polished index fingernail, she punched in four numbers so he could see them. "I don't know why you're digging around but don't be rude, okay?"

Carlos snorted. "She likes for everybody to be polite."

"Nothing wrong with manners," Julian said.

Though his voice was friendly, she didn't make the mistake of thinking that he was ready to accept her. Behind his glasses, his mesmerizing eyes narrowed slightly, reminding her of a cat playing with a mouse. Julian was arrogant—the type who'd allow her to make a move and lead her to hope that escape was possible before he knocked her over with a swipe of his paw. She wouldn't let her guard down. Angie wasn't anybody's easy prey.

She addressed the men at the table. "Time's short. I ought to get started right away."

Julian stood. "May I offer you a ride?"

Being alone with him in a car seemed risky, but she didn't have a choice. Murph wouldn't want to take her and calling a rideshare service for a pickup after a meeting with known criminals didn't seem prudent. "I don't need to wear a hood this time, do I?"

"I wouldn't want to hide that pretty face."

The fact that she managed to suppress her natural tendency to blush at his compliment was a testimony to her skill at falsehood. She was attracted to him but couldn't allow herself to be disarmed. She returned his fake smile with one of her own and followed him out of the boardroom.

In the underground parking structure, she took a quick inventory of parked vehicles that ranged from flashy sports cars to humble delivery vans like the one from Valentino's to a tanklike Hummer. Julian Parisi's high-end, silver SUV managed to combine the rugged power of an off-road vehicle with the luxe of a limo. The vehicle suited the man with starry blue eyes and muscular shoulders. He was tough and smart, a dangerous combo. She needed to figure out where Julian fit into the Lorenzo organization and why he'd been the one to offer her a ride.

She climbed into the passenger side and snuggled into the smooth leather seat that fit her like a very expensive glove. Passing the first hurdle and getting herself hired had been easy, but there would be more to come. She suspected that the Professor would be administering the next test, and failure could have lethal consequences.

With her seat belt fastened, Angie turned her head

and studied the man behind the steering wheel. *Damn, he's hot.* In profile, his features were chiseled. His dark blond hair gave the impression of being unkempt, but she figured that his style was the result of expensive barbering. He glanced toward her and quickly looked away, avoiding eye contact. *What are you hiding, Mr. Adonis?*

She asked, "We're headed back to my motel, right?"

"I think there's someplace else you'd rather go."

"Where's that?"

"You'll see."

She was wary and irritated. He had no right to make decisions for her. She glided her finger along the secret pocket in her bedazzled jeans where her switchblade was hidden. "I have a better idea. You tell me where we're headed, and I'll decide if it's okay."

"It's better than okay." He didn't seem threatening, but she'd heard that most sociopaths were charming. He continued, "When we get there, you can tell me if I'm right."

As they emerged from the garage and drove west, she tallied up the facts she'd learned today. The FBI dossier she'd been given for this assignment hadn't mentioned Julian Parisi—a gross oversight since he seemed to be a major player. The other men she'd met had been described with emphasis on Zapata, a high-ranking number cruncher who had a reputation for crunching bones when debts weren't paid on time.

She knew that the six-story square office building they'd just left was used mostly for accounting, real estate, investments and other relatively legitimate businesses. Most of Lorenzo's other enterprises were in central Denver, not the mountains. Where was Julian taking her?

After a long drive on the highway, the SUV exited onto a curving two-lane road that led deeper into the pine-covered foothills. Her anxiety kicked up. A seed of panic took root in her belly and sprouted branches as she remembered horror stories about fierce grizzly bears, rockslides and flash floods. Nature was dangerous. And the man behind the steering wheel might be equally lethal. He could throw her off a cliff or drown her in the rapids of a river. Since she was undercover, nobody would miss her…not for months.

Without inside info, she could only hope that he was a decent guy. In her undercover work, she'd run across many criminals—especially those involved in white-collar crime—who resembled corporate executives more than felons. They wore expensive clothes, had good taste and sent their kids to exclusive schools. Julian might be one of those guys…an MBA who took a wrong turn.

Or he could be a stone-cold killer.

Chapter Two

Angie fidgeted in the passenger seat. This drive seemed endless. "Here's a thought. You don't have to tell me where we're going, but I want to guess."

"Take your best shot."

"A restaurant?"

"There's food."

For an instant, hunger overwhelmed her anxiety. Coming from LA, she'd been driving for the past couple of days, living off burgers and chicken nuggets. "I wouldn't mind a nice meal."

"There's also dancing."

"A cowboy bar," she guessed, "with a mechanical bull."

"We're not going line dancing." The two-lane road swerved into a thick forest. The golden glow of sunset filtered through heavy boughs and dappled the scenery. "I'm taking you to a private gentleman's club."

A fancy name for a strip joint! In her teens when she was bouncing around in foster care and desperate for cash, she'd pole danced in one of those places that was supposed to protect the women who worked there. They didn't.

Why was he driving toward a place that was obviously inappropriate? This might be some kind of test, like being ordered to wear that black hood when Carlos was driving. Julian might think the degrading locale would show that her position in the Lorenzo family was precarious. Not that she needed a reminder. Living undercover with the constant threat of danger was growing more difficult with every assignment. "Take me back to my motel."

"We're almost to the club."

Rounding a twist in the road, the SUV came out of the forest. On the opposite side of a wide meadow, she saw a stone-and-cedar building with a flagstone terrace and a deck jutting from the front. Seven-story wings rose on either side of the center section. From the windows and rustic balconies, she guessed that the wings were used for hotel space. On the left end was a half-full parking lot. A neon sign over the entryway said Nick's. No doubt, Nick referred to Nicolas Lorenzo, the bastard who had taken Marigold.

A flood of emotions whirled inside her. She was scared about what might happen, excited for a new challenge and eager for revenge. Why hadn't her FBI handlers told her about this place? She covered with one word: "Impressive."

"Not what you expected?"

"Most of the gentlemen's clubs I've seen are super sleazy. This place is actually kind of wholesome."

"The times are changing."

"What's that supposed to mean?"

"Las Vegas advertises fun for the whole family. They've got roller coasters and water slides and petting zoos."

The gambling capital of the world looked like a touristy playground with activities for every age and taste, but that wasn't the Vegas she knew. Angie was more familiar with the dark underbelly where desperate gamblers squandered their last nickel, hookers offered group discounts and vice was readily available.

He pulled onto the shoulder of the road and parked. When he turned toward her, he took off his glasses and slipped them into the pocket of his blazer. "I know your secret, Angie. You're not who you say you are."

Masking her surprise, she hid within her undercover identity and got ready to avoid trouble by lying. Her deceptions followed a few simple rules: keep your adversary off-balance by confronting them; start with the truth—make the lie plausible; and reveal as little as possible. "Why would you say that?"

"Your online identity starts three years ago. Before that, you didn't exist."

She scoffed. "I thought professors were supposed to be smart."

"Why don't you explain it to me?"

"Obviously, I'm not using the name I was born with. In my line of work, I need to change my identity." She'd also transformed from a mousy brunette to a flashy platinum blonde but he didn't need to know that. "Three years ago, I wiped the slate clean."

"Does your line of work have anything to do with the feds?"

He leaned a few inches closer. Without the glasses, the shimmer in his eyes was nearly devastating, but she kept her focus. "Are you asking about Harris?"

"Maybe I am."

"Yeah, we dated, but as soon as he grew a tail and turned into a rat, I dumped him."

"Let me give you a warning, Angie. You seem like a decent person."

"Do I? That's not the look I was going for." With her long ponytail, red lipstick and studded jacket, she thought she'd been doing an excellent impersonation of Badass Barbie.

"Denver seems like an easygoing place where the kids play guitars and ride bikes and the sky is not cloudy all day. But don't underestimate the Lorenzo family. Once you're part of their business, it's hard to get out. Here's my advice to you, back away while you still can. Hop into your Toyota and drive back to California."

"I'm not a quitter." She'd studied the odds and figured that she had a shot at derailing a human trafficking operation, not to mention the possibility of taking revenge against Lorenzo for the disappearance of Marigold so many years ago. Her risk was worth the reward. "Is there food at your fancy gentlemen's club?"

"Four bars and three restaurants, one is gourmet."

She sensed there was something he hadn't told her. "What else?"

"This is where you'll be working. The OTB venue is on the lower level."

Surprise, surprise. She hadn't expected to be stashed away in the mountains. How was she going to dig into the inner workings of the Lorenzo organization from this remote location? Somehow, she needed to get back into the thick of the city.

Without another word, he started the engine and drove to the front entrance where a deferential valet took his car keys. Julian thanked the young man by name.

"You must come here often," she said.

"I ought to. I'm the general manager." He accompanied her to the front door, which another valet whipped open for them. "I don't handle the details of the day-to-day operations, but I oversee the building."

"Does that mean you're my supervisor?"

"No."

He was starting to annoy her. "You should have told me from the start that I'd be working here. Then, I wouldn't have spent the whole long, very long, drive worrying."

"Worrying about what?"

"For all I knew, you could be some kind of serial killer weirdo. And you could have been escorting me to a shallow grave where my bones would be picked clean by coyotes."

"How do you know I'm not?"

She took a moment to look around. "This place is too classy for a serial killer."

The large, three-story-tall lobby was an attractive space with flagstone floors and woven carpets. Rustic staircases on either side led to an upper level and downstairs. The tasteful decor combined antiques and heavy wooden furniture arranged around two moss rock fireplaces. A front desk for the hotel stretched along one wall.

He asked, "Are you still impressed?"

"There's more natural light than I would have expected."

"Glass ceiling." He looked upward at the A-frame skylight high above them. "A number of contractors told me that feature would never work, but it does. The other lighting is geared to create an open atmosphere."

He sounded proprietary, and that attitude made her wonder. "Did you build this place?"

"For the past three years, I've been working on renovations."

She pointed toward the balcony that encircled the second story. "What's up there?"

"There's a coffee shop and a bar that opens onto the deck. At the rear is a gourmet restaurant. Behind that is a members-only casino with poker, blackjack and roulette. No slots."

"I thought gambling was illegal, except in certain cities in Colorado."

"We get around the restrictions because Nick's is a social club. The gambling is a diversion we offer our members—not a significant part of our operation."

Halfway down the lobby to her right was the entrance to the strip club that she'd expected to find. A tasteful sign read Nick's Burlesque. At the closed door, two muscular bouncers stood guard and checked the ID's of a couple of guys in baseball caps. When the door opened, the echo of a country western song slipped out. She recognized the tune as "Save a Horse (Ride a Cowboy)." And she cringed at the unbidden memories of her time on the pole.

When she turned in the opposite direction, she recognized a tall, tanned man with silver hair combed back from his forehead. It had been eleven years since she'd seen him. Nick Lorenzo hadn't aged at all.

When Julian introduced them, she fought to hide her explosive surge of pure rage. She forced herself to shake his hand. "I've heard so much about you."

"Likewise." He treated her to a slow scrutiny. "Your hand is shaking."

"I must be hungry." She looked away, fearful that he'd see the hatred boiling inside her. She wanted to claw his face with her fingernails, to slash her blade across his carotid, but violence would only be a temporary satisfaction. Building a case against Lorenzo would be far better. She focused on her assignment. "I spoke to your man Zapata, and he gave me ten days to punch up your profits."

"I trust his judgment."

"You won't be disappointed."

She forced herself to confront him, eyeball to eyeball. The last time she'd seen Nicolas Lorenzo, she'd been a bow-legged, gawky fifteen-year-old with stringy brown hair and scraggly teeth in need of braces. He'd been so captivated by Marigold that he hardly noticed her. Now he was staring.

"Have we met before?" he asked.

It took all her considerable skill at deception to mask

the truth with flirtation. She flapped her fake eyelashes and gave a husky laugh. "I could never forget a man like you. Wealthy, powerful and…" she reached toward him with her painted fingernail and traced the lapel of his sports jacket "…and sexy."

Had she gone too far? She'd waited so long for vengeance that she was momentarily thrown off-balance. *Get it together.* She had to succeed in putting this snake out of business—for the sake of her best friend.

As soon as Angie and Lorenzo met, Julian sensed trouble. He observed them with the sort of morbid fascination usually reserved for the moment before a locomotive crashes into a stalled car on the railroad tracks. A major disaster was imminent, and he doubted that he could slam on the brakes. In the short time he'd been with Angie, he deduced that she wasn't a woman who backed down. She'd told him that she wasn't a quitter.

And Lorenzo was worse. If he got angry, there was no stopping him. In the three years it had taken to build Nick's, Julian had learned that his boss didn't listen to advice, even when the suggestions were prudent. Lorenzo ran his business based almost entirely on ego, and his instincts were often wrongheaded, especially when it came to women. If he considered them to be potential lovers, he rolled out the charm. If they were worker bees, he barely wasted a glance in their direction. Angie presented a problem for him because she didn't neatly fit either category. Not only was she pretty enough to be á lover but she came with a set of skills that would benefit the organization. And she was sending out mixed signals, licking her lips and flirting. Her voice was breathy when she claimed to be delighted by this opportunity to spend time with *Lorenzo the Great*.

Her sarcasm was too subtle for his boss who preened at being referred to as "Great." Julian guessed that in Lorenzo's one-track mind he thought he'd discovered a truly elusive, mythical creature: a woman who would make sweet love all night and earn money during the day. Before he could take a stroll down that fantasy lane, Angie sent him on a detour, talking about a mutual acquaintance in California who'd made a pass at her.

"Almost ripped his fingers off," she said with a too-loud laugh. Her pouty smile turned feral as her lips pulled back to bare her white teeth. "Nobody coerces me. Nobody commands me to do something I don't want to do."

Lorenzo took a backward step but didn't give up. "As long as you're going to be working here, I want you to stay in the hotel."

"Or maybe not." Julian wasn't thrilled with the idea of having Angie here all the time. He didn't know what game she was playing but was certain that she was trouble. "Most people don't like to live where they work."

"Not like you," Lorenzo said.

"What does that mean?" Angie asked.

"My man Julian is on the job night and day." He reached over and patted Julian's shoulder. The boss was one of those guys who liked to poke, stroke and jab… all in good fun. He continued, "When he first started working for me, he was nothing but a contractor in a hard hat and a tool belt. Look at him now. His blazer is tailored, and he's wearing eight-hundred-dollar custom-made boots."

Not true. Though Julian knew carpentry, he had training as an architect. And he didn't believe in throwing away money on clothes. He attempted to steer the conversation away from Angie's housing situation. "I was on my way downstairs to show Angie her new office."

"Wish I could join you," Lorenzo said, "but I have a business dinner. Angie, I insist that you stay in a hospitality suite on the fourth floor. You'll have daily maid service, access to 24/7 room service and a much better view than the parking lot of your cheesy motel."

"Thank you." She was cool and polite. "How could I say no?"

"I'll send Murph to pick up your luggage."

"Not Murph. I'd rather not have him pawing through my things."

"Of course not."

Lorenzo snapped his fingers toward the hotel reservations desk where Tamara Rigby was in charge. She glared as she came toward them, and Julian didn't blame her for being annoyed. Tamara was too qualified to be considered a worker bee. She had a degree in hospitality management and an MBA. Julian knew he was lucky to have her working here.

While she and Angie made arrangements to pick up her car and luggage from the motel, Julian contemplated how his afternoon had gone to hell. The downward trajectory started when he failed to convince Angie to quit. Then Lorenzo invited her to stay in one of the hospitality suites. And now, Tamara was shooting angry glares in his direction. He didn't think the day could get worse until Lorenzo said, "One more thing…"

Julian watched a young man with a beak-like nose, black hair and dark eyes shuffle across the lobby toward them. He wore a shoulder holster under his blazer. His name was Rudy Lorenzo.

While they shook hands, his uncle explained, "Rudy is moving into the office next to yours, Julian. He'll be your assistant."

"I like to do my own hiring. No offense, Rudy."

"This is a done deal," Lorenzo said. "My sister's son works for you."

Julian didn't want or need an assistant. He had efficiently delegated the major responsibilities at Nick's, and the place was a smooth-running machine that managed to provide access to several vices without actually breaking any laws. From the start, Julian had known that this delicate balance couldn't last forever, but he wasn't ready to give up control. Something big was coming, and he wanted to be in on it.

Nick Lorenzo clasped Angie's arm and planted a light kiss on her forehead. "You're invited to a cocktail party at my place on Saturday night. Wear something nice."

"I'll be there," she said through clenched teeth.

Her eyes flashed a warning that Lorenzo didn't see. The boss had already moved on, striding across the lobby to meet his dinner partner—the newly elected mayor of a nearby mountain town.

"Let's get to it," Rudy said, rubbing his hands together. "I'll hang with you guys."

"Not necessary," Julian said. "I'm showing Ms. D'Angelo around, and you're already familiar with the place."

"Yeah, I've spent time with the pole dancers and at the poker tables, but I ought to see the offices, especially the sports betting. I want to meet Leif Farnsworth, the ex-Bronco quarterback who runs that operation."

"It's late. He's probably gone for the day."

"So, does he have a sense of humor? Would he think it was funny if I called him by his nickname—Falling Leif? I mean, that's a hoot on account of he got sacked so many times."

For the first time in hours, Julian felt the tension lift. A real grin spread across his face when he contemplated the literal fallout when Rudy insulted the quarterback. Leif hated his nickname. Whenever anyone mentioned it, he threw whatever happened to be at hand—a stapler, a coffee cup or one of the smaller computer programmers. "You might want to rethink that plan, Rudy."

Before they could descend to the basement level, the door to the burlesque club opened a slit, and a skinny, young girl slipped out. When she spotted Julian, she ran across the flagstone floor, jumped into his arms, and wrapped her arms and legs around him.

He patted her back. "What's wrong, Cara?"

"My mom needs you. You gotta come right now."

He glanced at Rudy, who seemed confused, which just might be his usual state of mind. Nothing Julian could do to repair Lorenzo's nephew. Likewise, he couldn't immediately fix the problems that came with Angie. The woman was a puzzle that required concentration to assemble.

Cara came first. Her crisis took precedence over the other disasters of the day.

Chapter Three

The girl who clung tightly to Julian looked over his shoulder, and Angie caught her gaze. Though the kid couldn't have been more than seven or eight years old, her eyes expressed a sad resignation that was typical of a much older person. Angie knew that attitude, and she guessed that Cara had seen enough of life to understand how things worked and, more important, how to get what she wanted. The girl's tense lips and clenched jaw showed her stubborn tendencies. Again, Angie understood. When she was growing up, her foster parents and her teachers and her social workers often complained that she was willful and disobedient. *Of course I was! That's how I survived.*

She gave a wink, which Cara returned. They were kindred spirits. If Angie had been twenty years younger, they would have been buddies, pals and partners in crime.

Unlike Angie in her youth, this kid didn't look like she'd been physically abused. Her jeans and yellow turtleneck were clean. Her sneakers were neatly tied, and her shiny brown hair fell halfway down her back in two tidy braids. It took someone with a personal connection—someone like Angie—to see the neglect.

Cara needed attention. She'd bolted through the doors of the burlesque club at a time of day when most families were sitting down to a dinner of meat loaf and mashed potatoes. Did people actually do that anymore? Cara had made a beeline for Julian's arms. He was her target. Angie suspected that the girl had been waiting for Julian, watching through a crack in the door or from some other secret vantage point. The way she attached herself to him made it clear that she never wanted to let him go.

Still holding the kid, he returned to where Angie was standing. He spoke into Cara's ear. "Here's the problem. If I go into the club to talk to your mother, I can't bring you along. Kids aren't allowed inside."

"But I was already there."

"It's not appropriate. Don't make me lecture you, again."

Though he set Cara's feet on the floor, he couldn't break the connection. The kid latched on to his hand and pleaded. "Please, Julian, let me come with. I won't get in the way. I mean it, cross my heart and hope to die."

Angie heard echoes of her own misspent childhood and the many empty promises she'd made to authority figures. Cara was smart and clever. She might have a wealth of useful information she'd be willing to share… if Angie could make it worth her while. *A seven-year-old confidential informant?*

"I have a suggestion," Angie said. "You can leave Cara with me."

The kid's head whipped around so fast that her braids twirled. Cara focused hard, looking her up and down, sizing her up. "Who are you? Julian's new girlfriend?"

"I'm a new employee," Angie said. "I'll be working downstairs in OTB."

Cara nodded. "I like your jacket."

"Want to try it on?"

"Sure." She dropped Julian's hand. Apparently, he wasn't as appealing as shiny, pink rhinestones.

"It's settled," he said with palpable relief. "There's a coffee shop upstairs. I'll meet you there in a few minutes."

"Cool," Rudy said. "I'll go with Julian."

Angie had been so caught up in the unexpected appearance of Cara that she'd forgotten the big lug that Nick Lorenzo left with them. Not so for Julian. Without skipping a beat, he tapped Rudy's heavy shoulder and said, "Your job as my assistant starts now. You need to accompany Angie. This is her first time at Nick's. Show the lady around."

"You got it, boss."

"Don't call me boss." He turned to Cara. "Stay with Angie and do what she says."

Wearing the too-big jacket, she sashayed ten steps as though walking the runway at a Paris fashion show. She pivoted and gazed at Julian with her brown, Bambi-like eyes. "You better hurry. My mom needs you."

The little girl watched every step Julian took as he headed toward Nick's Burlesque. When he disappeared behind the doors, she exhaled a deep, heartfelt sigh that made Angie wonder if the kid wanted Nick to be her new daddy or her boyfriend. Either way, it was creepy.

In normal circumstances, Angie tried not to get involved in other people's problems, but Cara was different. The kid was bright and resourceful. She had the appealing waif act down pat, but Angie could give her a couple of pointers on how to manipulate the grown-ups. A cute smile was good for drawing people close and making them want to help you, but a quivering lower lip would melt their hearts.

Before they really started talking, Angie needed to get Rudy out of the way, and she had to find a place where she and Cara wouldn't be observed on the multitude of surveillance cameras she'd noticed at Nick's. She asked, "Are you hungry?"

Cara preened in the pink jacket. "I could go for some sushi."

"Seriously? You like raw fish? How old are you?"

"Seven and I just started second grade." She tugged on Angie's hand. "We can eat at the Gourmand restaurant. The chef knows me."

"That's okay by me," Rudy said, "as long as I ain't paying."

"Or we could do something else." From what Julian had said, it seemed obvious that Cara wasn't allowed free rein of Nick's. She might welcome an opportunity to explore. "Where's your favorite place? Not the casino because they'll chase you right out. And I'm guessing the shops are too pricy."

Rudy reminded her, "We don't have time for shopping. We're supposed to go to the coffee shop."

"I've never been good at taking orders." She exchanged a knowing glance with Cara. "Besides, I don't think Julian will mind if we take a look around."

"There's a barn behind the hotel," Cara said. "I really love the horses."

Perfect! A barn might be the only place on the premises that didn't have surveillance. "Rudy, I have a job for you. Please tell Julian that we went to check out the barn."

He balked, placing his considerable weight between them and the door. "I mean no disrespect, but the boss wants you to go to the coffee shop."

"No disrespect." Where did that attitude come from? She made a guess. "Have you been talking to Murph?"

"He told me you like things to be polite."

"And you get it. Good! We're going to be friends, Rudy." She flashed a smile—a drop of honey to catch this fly. "Look through the window. Pretty soon it's going to get dark. If we want to see anything, we should go right away."

"But the boss said—"

"Cara and I will take a quick look at the horses, and then we'll go to the coffee shop. Please tell Julian. Can you do that for me?"

Rudy looked across the lobby at the entrance to the Burlesque with eager eyes. Obviously, he'd rather be mingling with the scantily clad dancers than tromping through the horse barn. He gave a nod. "Yes, ma'am, I'll do it."

The "ma'am" struck an odd note of deference. Angie

figured she was only a few years older than Rudy. "Thank you."

She and Cara went out the front door, descended the three stairs from the verandah and followed the wide asphalt pathway to the right. The last rays of sunlight speckled the forested hillsides. The temperature was cool but not chilly enough that she needed her jacket. Angie inhaled a deep gulp of air that was so clean and crisp that she coughed. Maybe the mountains weren't so bad, after all.

Cara looked up at her with undisguised respect. Apparently, the little girl approved of the way she'd gotten what she wanted from Rudy. Angie grinned back at her. Children weren't her thing, but she might have to make an exception for this one.

"You handled him," Cara said.

"You could have done the same." Angie probably shouldn't encourage such willful behavior. She changed the topic. "Did you go to school this morning?"

"Sure did. In the afternoon, Mom picked me up. Usually, we go home and hang out until my babysitter shows up. She stays until my mom gets off work. I knew today was gonna be different as soon as I saw my backpack and sleeping bag. Mom brought me to work with her. She said I could sleep in her dressing room."

Angie wasn't familiar with the arrangements for this burlesque show, but she knew that most strip clubs didn't provide private rooms for the dancers. Cara's mom must be a star. "Tell me about your mother."

"Her name is Jane, and she goes by Calamity Jane

because she does Wild West stuff. She's really popular and has a bunch of fans."

Hence the dressing room. "Tell me about her act."

"It's really cool. She uses throwing knives and bull-whips. In one routine, she snaps her whip at one of the other dancers until all her clothes are off. I mean, *almost* all her clothes. Nobody gets totally naked at Nick's."

"Sounds like a reasonable policy."

"Uh-huh." Cara shrugged her skinny shoulders. "Julian has a lot of rules."

"Like what?"

"No kids backstage. No drugs allowed. No performers are allowed to go out on dates with the customers or the staff. Stuff like that."

Angie had heard that story before from other strip joints that touted their operations as a humanitarian effort for young women who were down on their luck. She wouldn't press Cara for details. Angie wasn't here to investigate the burlesque show, which sounded like a legit operation, especially when compared with human trafficking. "Where did your mom learn how to use a whip?"

"She grew up on a ranch. She's also a sharpshooter, but Julian has a rule about real guns at work. Sometimes, she'll bring one anyway and leave it in the car."

Calamity Jane sounded like a potentially dangerous stripper. No wonder Julian was quick to respond to her problems. "Did she bring a gun today?"

"I dunno."

The asphalt path rounded the south wing of Nick's

and led past a windowless cedar wall below five stories of hotel rooms. Angie wondered what kind of activities went on at this level where there were no windows. Was it the off-track betting operation or a walk-in vault or a secret, illegal casino? It might be a good place to hide victims of human trafficking. She and Cara strolled past a cellar door built into the rear section. Angie noticed two surveillance cameras. At Nick's, someone was always watching.

A delivery truck loaded with beer drove along a road beside the pathway and circled past them toward the rear of the building. Earlier, when she and Julian left his SUV at the front door, she'd seen the parking lot at the other end but not this road. She'd thought there was only one access, but a rear entrance made sense. With all the restaurants and bars, there had to be a steady stream of deliveries, plus garbage pickup and laundry services for the hotel. All this coming-and-going made a good cover for criminal activity.

The rustic landscaping at the front melted into a part-dirt and part-asphalt yard that was over fifty yards wide and stretched all the way around to the loading dock in back of the hotel. Cara grabbed her hand and pointed to a long building with a corral attached. "There's the horse barn. Right over there."

"I see it." Four other outbuildings of various sizes surrounded the area.

Cara tugged Angie's hand. "We gotta hurry. It's getting dark."

"There's time." Thus far, they'd been satisfying

Cara's demands. It was time for Angie to get some payback. "Can I ask you a couple of questions?"

The girl rolled her eyes. "Okay, but we've got to keep walking."

"Why do you think your mother was so upset?"

"She didn't say, but she told me to stay close to her and not go running off."

Angie came to a halt. She squatted down so she was eye to eye with Cara. She wasn't surprised that the kid had disobeyed but wanted to understand why. "Did your mom explain why she was breaking the rules and bringing you to work?"

Cara lowered her gaze and stared at the toes of her sneakers. "She doesn't have time to give me a bunch of reasons. She's a single mother, always tired. When she gives me an order, I'm not supposed to ask why. I just do it."

"But you didn't do what she said. First chance you got, you went running to Julian."

"I'm not stupid. I could see that Mom needed help, and Julian is good at fixing things."

"Was your mom scared?" When Cara pinched her lips together and shook her head, Angie could tell that she'd hit the bull's eye. Something had frightened Cara's mother. Angie asked, "Is it dangerous?"

"She asked me if I saw a man with a black beard and a scar on his forehead." She tugged again at Angie's hand. "There's nothing else. Let's go to the barn."

"First, I've got to tell you a secret. Okay, here it is. I don't much like horses. They're big, stinky, slobbery and not very smart." She shuddered. "When we get to the barn, don't expect me to pet these animals."

Cara rolled her eyes. "Now who's the big, ol' scaredy cat?"

"Am not." Somehow she'd fallen into a grade school conversation pattern. *Not good.* "Okay, maybe I am a teensy bit scared. Don't tell anybody."

As they approached the barn, Cara added a bounce to her step. She waved at a rangy man wearing jeans, a plaid shirt and a beat-up cowboy hat. His bowlegs didn't disguise the fact that he was limping. As they approached, Angie noticed the cowboy's black eye.

"That's Waylon," Cara said. "He's my friend."

"Hey, cutie-pie," Waylon said with a friendly wave. "Who's this lady?"

"Her name is Angie, and she's scared of horses."

So much for Cara's ability to keep a secret. Angie shook the cowboy's outstretched hand and said, "Pleased to meet you."

"Y'all don't need to be ashamed," he drawled. "Horses can be dangerous."

"Agreed."

"In my years of working on ranches, I've come to believe that the main reason for fear is unfamiliarity. If you let me take you out for a ride, you'll learn to appreciate these animals."

Inside the horse barn, she saw a row of six stalls on the left side and six on the right. A total of seven were occupied with horses that peered over the half doors. No doubt, the beasts were calculating how they could get her alone and trample her.

Cara bounced up to him. "Have you seen my friend, Gigi?"

"Nope."

"Who's Gigi?"

Cara rolled her eyes again. "He's gonna tell you that Gigi is imaginary, but she's really real. I met her a couple of weeks ago when I was picking up pinecones behind the barn. She was silly, told me she lived in the forest like a chipmunk. Then Mom called for me, and I had to go."

Angie had to wonder if the imaginary playmate was somehow involved with human trafficking. This topic deserved further conversation, but not right now. Cara was on edge, and Angie didn't want to set her off. "We'll look for her."

"Good." She whirled and glanced up at Waylon. "Can I saddle up and take a ride?"

"Afraid not," Waylon said. "It's almost bedtime for these ponies."

"Can I feed them?"

"You know where the apples are. But you better take off that fancy jacket. With all those sparkles, the horses might think you're wearing their dessert."

She peeled off the pink rhinestone jacket and tossed it toward Angie, who was grateful to Waylon for rescuing her clothing from a bath in horse slobber. She watched as Cara dragged a small bench toward one of the stalls, grabbed an apple and fed the big brown horse. Then she petted the muscular neck and cooed.

Angie looked around the barn. She didn't see any cameras, but still she worried that they were under surveillance. Cameras were everywhere. Her earlier thought that they might avoid surveillance in the barn was wishful thinking.

"Are the guests at the hotel allowed to ride the horses?"

"Someday, we might have a program for horseback rides, but right now, they're private property and belong to Mr. Lorenzo."

That gave her another reason to dislike the beasts. The smarmy presence of Nick Lorenzo hung over every part of this place like an ominous, dangerous thundercloud. Her hatred for him had grown after seeing him again today. She'd almost forgotten the permanent sneer to his mouth and the greasy smugness that radiated from him.

She phrased her comments carefully. "It looks like you have room for expansion. What are all these outbuildings used for?"

"Mostly storage, and there's a garage for ATVs, snowmobiles and the Jeep we use for a snowplow in winter." He pointed toward a long, ranch-style building at the back of the lot. "That's a bunkhouse. In the summer, I usually have ten cowboys working for me. In this season, I only need five or six part-timers, and everybody goes home at the end of the day."

A vacant bunkhouse would be an ideal place for holding the victims of human trafficking. They could be brought here and tucked away until arrangements were made for their final destination. But was Waylon the sort of man who would go along with that scheme? He seemed kind and decent, but her radar for detecting villains wasn't working well. From the moment when she gazed into Julian's azure eyes, she'd been willing to believe that he had more in common with a smart, handsome professor than an upper-level thug in Lorenzo's operation.

She watched as Cara moved her bench to the next stall and greeted a black horse with a blaze of white on his forehead. She motioned for Angie to join her. "Come on, you can feed him the apple."

"No thanks." She put on her jacket, glad for the rhinestone armor to protect her from horses and other dangerous creatures.

"Are you going to be working here?" Waylon asked.

"I think she should be a performer at the Burlesque," Cara said.

Oh, hell no. But she didn't want to say anything that would insult Cara's mother. "I don't have any special talents."

"But you're pretty," the little girl said.

"Can't argue with that," Waylon said. "You're pretty enough to be a headline stripper."

Cara hopped off the bench, stamped her foot and glared at him. "How many times do I got to tell you? They're not strippers. They're performers."

Angie shot her a thumbs-up.

Waylon touched the brim of his hat in a sign of respect. "I'll try to remember. Young lady, it appears to me that you've got one more horse to feed."

While Cara got back to her task of distributing apples, Angie looked up at the cowboy. "That's quite a shiner you've got. What happened?"

"Tripped and fell into a fence post." He shifted his

weight from foot to foot, then he looked up and to the right—a nonverbal sign that he was lying…or trying to. He wasn't good at deception. "Guess I'm just clumsy."

"Is that when you hurt your leg? I saw you limping."

"Must have been at the same time." He hobbled across the barn toward Cara. "I don't rightly recall."

"Maybe you had a concussion. Did you get checked out by a doctor?"

"I ain't got no need for doctoring. Besides, I'd have to drive all the way into Denver. It's too far and a waste of time."

And Waylon wouldn't want a doctor to examine him and discover other bruises that showed he'd been in a brawl. "Aren't there local clinics?"

"This here is a small mountain county without a lot of special services."

Also, she figured, there probably wasn't much of a police presence. Nick's was a nearly perfect location for transporting illegal goods. They were close to Denver but separated by county lines that limited jurisdiction and investigation from big-city law enforcement.

When she took on this assignment, she thought she'd need to spend a couple of weeks investigating the organization and determining the location that would be used for trafficking. Her intuition told her that there was no need to look any further. The trafficking operation was certainly being funneled through Nick's. She'd fallen right into the middle of Lorenzo's spiderweb.

She was determined to put an end to it…an end to him.

Chapter Four

The snapping of two bullwhips—louder than gunfire—echoed against the silver striped walls inside Nick's Burlesque. Calamity Jane was dressed in a denim thong, a holster, a skimpy fringed vest and red cowboy boots. She'd already taken off her red cowgirl hat, and her curly brown hair bounced around her shoulders as she went through her routine with a whip in each hand.

Julian watched impatiently. Not that Jane's act was boring. She took aim at beer cans on a ledge onstage. One by one, she tore through them while never losing the beat to "American Woman." After a strut down the spotlighted runway, she used her whips to extinguish candles on two of the tables close to the stage. The small but enthusiastic audience applauded. Most of these guys had seen the show before and knew what was coming. They cheered when Jane pulled three wooden targets onto the stage and drew one of the throwing knives from her holster. Other knives awaited her on a special table. After a sexy bump and grind, she took aim at the first target that outlined the shape of a man. Three throws. *Thunk-thunk-thunk.* Three hits. Head, heart and crotch.

She was deadly accurate. He couldn't imagine that Jane was afraid of anything, but Cara had implied fear when she told him that her mom needed him. Julian would stand on his head to help Jane out, definitely didn't want to lose her. She was a draw, one of the most popular acts at the Burlesque. She'd worked at some of Lorenzo's other clubs in Denver but preferred Nick's because of Julian's rules prohibiting full nudity and fraternization with the customers. Some of the other dancers didn't mind showing more skin and picking up bigger tips. Not Jane. She'd told him that being a good mother was the most important thing in her life. She adored Cara.

The kid was bright, no doubt about that, and she had ten times the street smarts of most adults. That little girl had been clever enough to know that her mom couldn't chase after her while she was onstage. Cara must have waited for that precise moment before running out the door of Nick's Burlesque. This marked the third time he'd caught Calamity Jane bringing her daughter to work, and he couldn't let it slide.

Julian made his way around the club to the stage door, where he slipped inside. From the stage, he heard renewed cracking from Jane's whips. At an outdoor event, he'd seen her light a couple of specially treated whips on fire which made a spectacular effect in the darkness but was against regulations for the club. Near a long backstage table covered with a sparkling array of makeup and glitter, he motioned to Lola—a tall brunette in a flamenco-style dress who had a surprisingly operatic mezzo-soprano voice.

"I know why you're here," Lola said as she adjusted the ruffled skirt that she'd rip off during her aria from *Carmen*. "It's Cara, right?"

"Bringing a minor child to the club is against the rules."

"Maybe those rules ought to change. I've got a couple of kids myself, and I'd be willing to pay if you set up some kind of day care."

"Not a chance." Was she blind? Couldn't she see the obvious? Nick's was an adult establishment with drinking, gambling and sexy performers. Though he wanted to believe that these were victimless crimes, he knew that lines sometimes got blurred. People got drunk. Fights broke out. "I can't guarantee it would be safe, even if the day care was in a separate area."

"Why not?" Lola tapped him on the chest with the long-stemmed paper rose she always held between her teeth during her performance of the "Pole Dance of the Toreador."

"Number one, our patrons don't want to be bothered by children. Number two, this isn't a good environment for kids. And number three, I'm glad you feel like you can come to me with your concerns, but I'm not your caretaker. I'm your employer."

"So?"

"No day care, Lola. Now, tell me what Cara is so upset about."

"No idea. She probably just wanted to get your attention."

He hoped that was the only issue. The sooner this situation was taken care of, the sooner he could get back to Angie. She was up to something, and he needed to figure out what was going on. Her background references from sources in California didn't tell the whole story about Ms. D'Angelo. She'd already admitted that she erased her past and gave herself a new identity. What else was she hiding?

He heard the sound of Jane's act coming to a close with a flurry of swirling whips. She dashed backstage holding her red cowgirl hat filled with tips. As soon as she caught her breath, she confronted him. "I know you're mad."

"Yes."

"I can explain."

The backstage area offered zero privacy. In addition to the dancers and crew milling around, there were hidden cameras and mics, supposedly for the protection of the performers but the surveillance also gave an insight into potential hustles these ladies could be planning. No cameras in the bathrooms, but there was audio surveillance. The three private dressing rooms, including Jane's, were discreet. He followed her into the room and closed the door. The scent of leather from her whips and holster mingled with a woodsy perfume.

"I'm listening," he said.

"Just before I went onstage, somebody told me that Cara ran off, and I'm guessing she went looking for you. Where is she?"

"Don't worry. I left her with a reliable adult."

"Are you sure this person is responsible?"

There were a number of reasons that Angie couldn't be trusted, but Julian couldn't imagine that she'd harm a child. "She's a new hire, assigned to revamp the OTB operation."

"You left her with a woman? Good! Cara tends to get attached to men. She sees all of them as potential father figures, but I don't have to tell you that."

Jane unfastened her holster and hung it on a peg before she stepped behind a screen to change. Not wanting to accidentally ogle, he trained his gaze on a photo of Jane and Cara that sat on her dressing table. They were riding on a sorrel horse with mountains in the background. "You can't keep bringing her to work."

"I'm sorry."

He noticed that the apology didn't come with a promise to never do it again. "Cara said you needed my help. What's going on?"

"I saw something I probably shouldn't have, and now this jackass is following me. I don't recognize him." She was babbling, nervous. "He's got a dark beard and a scar on his forehead. Does he work here? I'm sure there's a simple explanation. Maybe he just got a job in one of the kitchens?"

Her obvious tension worried him. Jane wasn't the sort of woman who got easily frightened. "What was the jackass doing?"

"I don't want to get anybody in trouble." She poked her head out from behind the screen. "Can you promise that you won't fire anybody or put them on leave or dock their pay?"

"I'll do whatever is necessary if there's real danger. Tell me what you saw."

She dove back behind the screen. When she emerged,

she was wearing jeans and a plaid flannel shirt. Except for the glitter and exaggerated stage makeup, she looked like somebody who worked at a ranch. "Yesterday, I got here early and went out to the barn. Waylon lets me take the horses out for a run so they'll get exercise. When I was getting back, I heard a commotion from inside the horse barn. Somebody with a deep voice yelled a bunch of threats."

"Do you remember what was said?"

"A whole lot of cursing and stuff like, 'You'd better not tell. Keep quiet or else.'"

"What were they supposed to keep quiet about?"

"I don't know." She plunked down in the chair at her dressing table to put on her sneakers. "I rode closer. That's when I spotted this guy storming away. If I'd been armed, I would have nailed him. But I got distracted by what I saw in the barn. Waylon was bleeding and struggling to stand. He'd been hurt bad, and I rushed to help him."

Jane shuddered, clearly upset by this incident. Later today, Julian could check yesterday's video from the horse barn. "Did Waylon tell you what the fight was about?"

"He said it was just a scuffle, told me to forget I'd ever seen that guy. And I probably would have done that. But this afternoon I saw him again. Oh, damn, what am I going to do?" She dabbed under her eyes with a tissue, wiping away tears before they fell and smudged her mascara. "He was standing on the sidewalk across the street from my house in Denver. He knows where I live, where my daughter goes to school."

"Did he say anything?"

"I didn't give him the chance. I picked Cara up from school and drove here." She looked up at him. "What if he comes after us?"

"Is there anybody else you told about this?"

She shook her head, sending ripples through her brown curls. "I told Cara to watch out for a guy with a beard and a scar, but I didn't want to talk to anybody until I knew what was going on. Julian, what should I do?"

"You and Cara stay here tonight on the concierge level."

"Is it safe?"

"The guys who work on that level are trained bodyguards, former Marines."

"That means they're sharpshooters."

"They'll protect you." He rested his hand on her shoulder. "And if the first line of defense fails, you've got your guns, your knives and your whips. You'll be fine."

"Why did that man with the scar come after me?"

"I'm not sure." *A giant understatement.* He was aware that something big was going down in the next couple of weeks, but Nick Lorenzo hadn't seen fit to brief him on the details. Julian was responsible for what happened at Nick's but knew very little about the rest of Lorenzo's operations.

He hoped the man with the scar was nothing more than a bully with a grudge against Waylon, hoped their fight had no deeper significance. But he suspected deeper problems were on the horizon. The gentlemen's club was relatively successful but didn't make massive profits, not even with the casino. Sooner or later, Lorenzo would get greedy. There would be demands.

He heard a heavy knock on the dressing room door. "Can I come in?"

It was Rudy. His uncle Nick had probably assigned this kid to be Julian's assistant so that Rudy could keep an eye on him. Trouble was in the air. "Get in here."

Rudy stuck his head inside. His heavy, dark eyebrows raised and his beak of a nose twitched from side to side as if sniffing. "Hi, Miss Jane."

"Howdy," she drawled. "What are you doing here?"

"You're going to be seeing a lot of me. I'm Julian's new assistant."

Julian stepped toward him. "You were supposed to be watching Angie." He purposely avoided mention of Cara. The last thing he needed was an explosion from Calamity Jane.

"Don't worry, boss. Everything is okay." He swaggered into the dressing room, hitched his thumbs in his pockets and surveyed the whips, knives and skimpy, sparkly outfits. "Anytime there's trouble backstage, Miss Jane, you can call on me to help. I'm your man."

"Angie was supposed to wait for me in the coffee shop," Julian said.

"Well, sir, she and Cara changed their minds. They went to see the horses before it got dark."

Jane bolted to her feet. "My daughter is at the horse barn?"

"Yes, ma'am."

"The one place I told her *not* to go."

She darted from the room and headed toward the rear exit. Julian followed.

Rudy brought up the rear. "Did I do something wrong?"

"You've seen Jane's act," Julian said. "Once I saw her snap the buttons off her boyfriend's jeans with her whip because she thought he was cheating on her. You'd better hope nothing bad happened to her kid. Run and keep up with her."

Rudy blew past him like a nervous tornado.

Chapter Five

With his phone pressed to his ear, Julian made his way through the back hallways of Nick's. His first call was to Tamara Rigby to check on the progress of picking up Angie's luggage and to reserve a suite on the concierge level for Jane and Cara. Then he called the concierge desk to alert them to the arrival of new guests. Then he contacted the tech expert in the surveillance room and asked him to pull up footage of the horse barn for the last two days. He slipped his phone into an inner pocket of his blazer. The situation was under control.

He exited through a door by the loading dock where cases of beer were being off-loaded. A dark blue van for Valentino's Bakery and Wedding Cakes nestled into a parking spot by the kitchen door, which didn't necessarily mean that fresh bread was being delivered. Valentino the Baker preferred using his vans for personal transportation. If the Baker was here, he might be dining with Nick Lorenzo. Julian reminded himself that he needed to move fast if he hoped to catch the big boss and get some straight answers, assuming that Lorenzo would be honest with him. *Not good odds on that bet.*

A cluster of kitchen workers gathered at a picnic table by the fence to taste the beer and have a smoke. The normal bustle at Nick's seemed to be moving forward at an unperturbed pace, but he sensed undercurrents of trouble.

Night had fallen. The outdoor LED lights spread illumination across the asphalt road and parking area. Julian strode toward the horse barn. After working three years at Nick's, he'd become more than a manager. He'd learned to walk a fine line between efficiency and empathy. His duty was to keep the various businesses running, but he cared about the people who worked for him and their needs. Lorenzo warned that Julian was too approachable, too soft. Lola felt comfortable about demanding a day care center. Jane confided in him. Waylon needed his protection.

Julian couldn't turn away, but he couldn't hold this delicate balance forever. Sooner or later, he'd have to leave Nick's. But not today…today he worked for Nick Lorenzo and was doing a good job.

As he approached the barn, a tableau unfolded under the lights outside the open double doors. Jane squatted down in front of Cara, alternating hugs and kisses with severe scolding. Rudy rested his hand on his shoulder holster and scanned in all directions, obviously looking for something to shoot. Waylon pulled down the brim of his hat to hide the bruises on his face. And then, there was Angie in her sparkly pink jacket with her long platinum ponytail draped behind her like a flag. Her slender fingers covered her lips, and he had the distinct impression that she was holding back laughter.

When she spotted him, she gave a nod of recognition and a conspiratorial grin, as if to say: *Good luck with this mess, glad it's you and not me.* She tapped Cara on her skinny little shoulder and pointed out that Julian was almost here. All eyes turned toward him.

He inhaled, breathing in the scent of hay and horses that reminded him of his youth in Wyoming. He pushed his glasses up on his nose and inserted himself into the scene.

"Are you okay, Cara?"

She bobbed her head. "I'm good."

"Jane?"

She positioned herself behind her daughter, holding Cara to keep the girl from dashing off somewhere. "Thanks, Julian. We're going to be fine."

"You and Cara will stay here tonight. I just talked to the guys on the concierge level, and they have a suite for you. Order room service from any of the restaurants."

"Can I get anything I want?" Cara asked.

He imagined the little princess calling for platters of sushi and lobster followed by ice cream sundaes. "Your mom will place the order."

"I really appreciate this," Jane said. "Before we get settled for the night, I ought to go backstage to pick up a few things."

"It's better if you and Cara go directly to your room and stay there. Rudy will escort you. If you need anything, tell the guy at the concierge desk, and he'll take care of it."

The five bodyguards who shared the concierge duties were among his most trusted employees. Using their training as former Marine sharpshooters and experts in hand-to-hand combat, they kept the concierge floor safe for those who might be in peril. On the flip side, they might also be called upon to contain Lorenzo's enemies. On one occasion, they spent a week guarding an ex-wife who needed to be removed from the property and sent far away. Sometimes, Nick Lorenzo extended hospitality to other crime organizations and cartels that were represented by dangerous people—animals that couldn't be left unchecked.

This particular assignment—guarding Jane and Cara—was a winner for the concierge team. Julian was fairly sure that his bodyguards would be happy to spend time with Calamity Jane. They could exchange tips on gun handling and whips.

"What about Angie?" Cara asked. "Is she going to stay with us?"

"She'll also have a room on the concierge level. After I finish showing her around, I'll bring her upstairs." He shot Rudy a glance. "Make sure they get to their suite."

"I'm on it." He herded Jane and Cara toward Nick's.

Julian's first problem was solved: Jane and Cara were no longer in harm's way. Next, he needed to find out why the man with the scar had attacked the old cowboy. Julian glanced toward the barn door. Waylon had disappeared. Why? Was he hoping to avoid the inevitable conversation? Julian muttered, "Where the hell did he go?"

"He's back by the horse stalls," Angie said. She placed her hand on Julian's forearm as if she could restrain him with a touch. "Waylon probably doesn't want to talk about getting beat up. It's embarrassing to admit, especially to the boss. Not that it's any of my business."

"You're right about that." He patted her hand and deliberately removed it. "What happens between me and my employees is not your problem."

His plate was full. He had a load of other things to worry about, including the sexy blonde who stood beside him. He wasn't sure he should be talking in front of Ms. D'Angelo until he knew her real identity. Was she going to mess up everything he'd worked so hard to build? Creating this gentlemen's club hadn't been easy. Now that everything was up and running, he hated to see it fall apart.

Turning away from her, he took a stride toward the horse barn. Getting rid of Angie wouldn't be easy. She fell into step beside him. "Waylon hasn't done anything wrong. He told us that he feels terrible about putting Jane and Cara in danger."

"Maybe you should wait out here."

"If there's really any danger, I'd rather not stand outside like a pink rhinestone target," she said. "Don't worry. I won't get in the way."

Since she'd already heard everything Cara, Jane and Waylon had to say, there wasn't much point in trying to keep her out of the loop. Inside the barn, he approached the old man. "If you don't mind, Waylon, I want to see your face."

Reluctantly, he took off his hat. Gray hair matted on his forehead, and his complexion was waxy and pale. The dim light inside the barn masked his bruises, but he still looked like he'd wrestled with a lawn mower.

His left eye was black-and-blue. His jaw was swollen. Bandages covered a couple of cuts on his face, and he'd hidden any damage to his hands with worn leather work gloves.

He lifted his chin and said, "My noggin got banged around, but it ain't bad."

"Did you go to a doc?"

Waylon shook his head. "I don't need anybody poking and prodding and taking X-rays. I'm okay."

"Stubborn," Julian said under his breath. "Here's the deal, Waylon, I can't force you to seek medical attention, but I strongly suggest it. In the meantime, you're taking two days off with pay, starting now."

"No, sir, that doesn't work for me. I'm starting a new project."

"What project?"

"Me," Angie said. "Waylon agreed to give me horseback riding lessons."

"I thought you hated horses."

"I do. This is an opportunity to get over my fears. I mean, as long as I'm running the off-track betting operation, I should know something about the animals."

Her logic made sense. Apparently, Waylon agreed, because he puffed out his chest and braced himself to take a stand. Julian had bigger things to worry about. "Fine, you two can plan your timing for Angie's horseback riding lessons, but I still want Waylon to take off two days at least. The other cowboys can fill in for you."

"Then it's settled," Angie said as she headed for the door. "Let's get back to our tour of Nick's. I can't wait to see my office."

"I'm not done," Julian said. "I have a couple of questions for Waylon…if you don't mind."

"Sorry for the interruption."

She was polite; he had to give her credit for that. Bossy *and* polite made a dangerous combination. He couldn't get mad at her but couldn't allow himself to be railroaded. She took a step backward and went silent as though she could fade into the woodwork. *Impossible!* No matter how hard she tried, this flashy woman would never be invisible.

He turned to the battered cowboy. "What was the fight about?"

"I caught the guy sneaking around by the garage and told him this area was off-limits and he needed to leave. I thought he might be a member of the club so I was careful not to be rude. He seemed to understand, gave me a nod and took off. But he wasn't gone, not for long. About an hour later, I saw him again. This time, I yelled for him to get away from here, and I might have cussed a little."

"Was anybody with him?" Julian asked.

"Not that I could tell."

"Did he give you his name?"

"He did not, and I never saw him before."

"After you yelled the second time, what happened?"

"He came after me like a rabid badger, charged into the barn and started throwing punches. I'm not much of a fighter, but I could tell that this guy knew where to hit and make it hurt. He slammed me up against the stalls and kept hollering about how I better not tell anybody about this or else. That's when Jane rode up, and the guy took off." His hesitant eye contact was both sad and courageous. "That son of a bitch better not try to hurt her."

"Don't worry about Jane and Cara. Nothing bad is going to happen to them. I'm more concerned about you, Waylon. Maybe you ought to stay in Denver with your sister."

"I won't bring trouble to her doorstep," he said. "My cabin is safe. I've got alarm systems and firearms. The guy with the scar got the jump on me once. Ain't going to happen twice."

Julian realized that Angie had analyzed the situation perfectly. Waylon felt responsible for Jane being threatened, and he was more embarrassed than hurt. "Next time—if there is a next time—I want you to call me first thing. Now, you should head on home."

"I was just about to do that. Larson is working the night shift, and he ought to show up real soon."

"You go," Julian said. "We'll wait until Larson gets here."

Before Waylon left, Angie gave him a hug and promised to call about the riding lessons. Then she joined Julian to watch as the old cowboy limped across the grounds to an area where cars were parked. "You handled that well," she said.

"I have my moments."

He strolled outside and led her to the whitewashed corral fence attached to the barn. Standing here in the shadows, he could look up and see the stars coming out. Nightfall in the mountains was amazing and beautiful. The inky black sky filled with stars—a thousand times more than were visible in a city. To the east, the glow from Denver's lights was visible. He pointed to a bright star. "That's Vega. Behind that is the jaw of Draco the dragon. That square shape to the north is supposed to be the body of Pegasus the flying horse."

"Where's Scorpio?" she asked. "That's my birth sign."

"I don't know." He wasn't into astrology and not an expert in astronomy, either. He just liked stargazing. "When I was growing up in Lander, Wyoming, me and my brother sat on the porch every night after dinner. He'd play his guitar, and I'd look up and dream about the future."

"Did your dreams come true?"

Not yet. He looked down at her face…so beautiful in the starlight. This conversation had gotten too personal for his taste. He needed to keep his distance from her… and everybody else for that matter. "So, Angie, do you have any questions?"

"Tons," she said. "Where do you want to start?"

"Give me something easy."

"I think I already know the answer to this one. Waylon was assaulted, but it doesn't sound like anybody contacted the local police."

She had to be kidding! According to her résumé, Angie had worked for other crime organizations in California and Nevada. She wasn't naive, couldn't possibly think they'd knowingly invite a cop into their house. "We prefer to deal with lawbreakers ourselves."

"That's what I thought. While we're on the topic of investigating, I noticed cameras in the lobby and also here in the horse barn. Do you have eyes and ears everywhere?"

"I do," he said without apology. "And my equipment is state-of-the-art. The cameras out here are designed to keep an eye on the horses and the expensive machinery in the garage." As soon as he had the chance to get to his surveillance room, he'd rewind backward in time to the fight with Waylon. If he was lucky, he'd be able to figure out what the man with the scar was looking for. "Surveillance is necessary. Nick's has a lot of cash businesses, especially with the casino. We need to be able to check what comes in and what goes out."

"Are there cameras in the hotel?" she asked.

"In every hallway." He could guess what she really wanted to know. "Don't worry about privacy. Nobody is going to take pictures of you in your room."

"It wouldn't be the first time." Her full, ruby-red lips frowned at what had to be a bad memory. "I don't like being spied on."

"Nobody does. Next question."

"Is Nick's open all night?"

"We sure are. Since we're a private club, we're not hampered by rules that govern other establishments. Some of the restaurants and the burlesque show close at midnight, but nobody wants to shut down a casino or pull the plug on a high stakes poker game when somebody else is losing big."

"What's your game?" she asked.

"Don't have one."

"Come on, Julian. Everybody has a favorite. Blackjack?"

She didn't know him, didn't know his background and didn't realize the significance of what she'd just said. Angie had just stepped over the line into forbidden territory. Julian didn't gamble and didn't drink. He'd lost four years of his young life to addiction and never wanted to relapse. Though he no longer attended AA meetings, he'd been sober for six years.

He stepped away from the corral. "Here comes Larson. I'll fill him in, and we can finish our tour."

He could feel the intense focus of her dark eyes as she walked beside him. "Something wrong?"

He didn't respond. This was his life and his problem. He didn't let anybody climb inside his head and poke around, especially not a pretty California girl with a mysterious past.

She gazed up at him. "Was it something I said?"

He tapped the face of his watch. They were wasting time. He had things to do, places to go. "I'm running late."

"No problem, I'm capable of exploring by myself."

Not a chance. He didn't want Angie wandering through the hotel, stirring up trouble. "I'll contact Tamara to finish your tour. When you get to your room, feel free to order anything from room service."

"Will I see you later?"

He didn't trust himself to visit her suite late at night when she'd changed from her sparkly jacket into a silky gown and unfastened her long, straight, platinum hair. "Tomorrow. If you have a problem, call me."

Switching into high gear, he briefed Larson, rushed to the hotel front desk and turned Angie over to Tamara. He entered his office on the second floor, closed the door, leaned against it and exhaled a long, ragged breath. She'd gotten inside his defenses and tweaked his nerves. And she'd done it so easily, as though she made a regular habit of shredding a man's life and skipping off to a riding lesson with her ponytail swinging behind her.

He went through the stack of papers on his desk. By the time he was done with the sorting, shuffling and signing, Julian felt like he was more in control. He put in a call to Nick Lorenzo, failed to reach him and left a text. Talking to Nick might give him all the answers he needed about the man with the scar.

Down a short hallway, Julian entered the surveillance room where dozens of camera feeds showed the activities taking place at Nick's. Gordon, the tech genius who helped build this system, sat in the midst of these screens and flashing lights. He swiveled his bobble head on his skinny neck and looked up at Nick. "What do you want to see?"

"The cameras at the barn and surrounding area. I need to go back two days." He gave Gordon an idea of what to look for. "There have been reports of a man with a scar lurking around in that area. I want to see where he goes and what he's after. Also, let's zoom in for a tight close-up so we can use our facial recognition software."

"Give me a minute."

Julian took a seat. There was a bit of private business he wanted to handle. When he'd told Angie that there would be no secret photos of her, he'd meant it. But there were, in fact, two cameras and mics in her bedroom suite. He punched a series of buttons to access those cameras. His intention was to shut them down… but there was no harm in taking a peek…just to be sure she was all right.

Both screens were dark.

He checked the microphones. Dead.

A spark of panic fired up inside him. He didn't want to believe that something bad had actually happened to her. The problem had to be in the equipment. "What's going on with this thing?"

Gordon popped up at his elbow. "Let's run it backward and see what's up."

They went back five minutes, then eight and then he saw Angie. She gazed directly into the lens of the camera and held up a sheet of hotel stationery with a message scrawled in lipstick. "Bye, bye, bye."

Gordon snorted a laugh. "I like her."

"I'll let you check out her phone and return it to her."

Angie reached up with the lipstick and painted over the camera lens.

Julian stared at the darkened screen and shook his head. *I like her, too.*

Chapter Six

After spending two days reinforcing her cover story by digging through spreadsheets, calculating algorithms and reprogramming computer software in her OTB office, Angie was eager to get out of the windowless basement at Nick's and attend a party. The occasion was the sixtieth birthday of Nolan Zapata, and lots of important people from Lorenzo's shady businesses all across Denver and the surrounding area would be there. Mingling with this crowd might shed light on her investigation, which was something she desperately needed.

Since her work in OTB relied on computer data, she had access to cyber records for Lorenzo's businesses. She'd hacked, studied and scanned but had found nothing definite about the size of the human trafficking operation, how it worked and when it was supposed to start. A few disturbing threads of data connected Lorenzo with coyotes known for transporting illegal immigrants and with a cartel involved in the sex trade. One of the main players in that cartel was named Zapata—just like Lorenzo's chief number cruncher.

She'd expected to find more details about payments.

Trafficking in human beings required negotiation and cooperation. There should have been more records and detailed plans, but her cyber search had been mostly futile. Tonight at the party, she planned to sneak into Lorenzo's office and download data from his personal computer onto a flash drive—a risky scheme. She had a better chance of getting info by chatting up Lorenzo's associates at the cocktail party. If she played her cards right, she might get these guys to blab about the impending operation.

One thing was for sure: that blabbermouth was *not* Julian. During the time he'd spent with her over the past couple of days, he'd been funny, polite and—*God help me!*—sexier than any man had a right to be. He'd told her nothing. She wasn't sure what it would take to make him open up to her. Maybe they'd never connect. Maybe she'd finally met the man who could resist her teasing and her lies.

Until she had details, there was no point in contacting the local FBI. She had to know enough to catch Lorenzo's guys in the act, which meant keeping her eyes and ears open at Zapata's birthday party. Tamara Rigby, also invited, advised her to dress up—the glitzier the better. But Tamara showed up at the door to Angie's suite on the concierge level wearing a blah cocktail dress with long, lacy sleeves. The beige of her dress was almost an exact match for her straight, chin-length hair.

When she looked at Angie, her eyes popped. "Wow."

Angie's jumpsuit was glistening white, strapless and streaked with gold threads. Her jacket and belt were metallic gold. She'd twisted her long platinum locks into a knot on top of her head which was fastened in place with decorative hair chopsticks, one of which doubled as a weapon. The other was a lockpick. "Am I overdressed?"

"You're perfect. I'm the one who needs sprucing up."

"No problem." She went to her closet and selected a curve-hugging red sheath with a plunging neckline. "You can't go wrong with red."

Tamara hesitated for less than a minute. "Do you think it'll fit?"

"I'm sure it will." Angie grabbed the dress and led Tamara into the landing outside her room where one of the hunky bodyguards sat behind the concierge desk. After a wave to him, she knocked on the door to Jane and Cara's suite.

As soon as Jane opened the door, Angie said, "We have a problem. Tamara needs to get totally glam before Julian picks us up in fifteen minutes."

Jane welcomed them inside. "You came to the right place. Come with me, Tamara. We'll start with your makeup."

"Shouldn't I try on the dress first?"

"That comes after I fix your face. I don't want to get makeup on your clothes."

Jane escorted her to the big mirror outside the bathroom, sat her down on a dainty little stool and flipped open a makeup box with a rainbow array of highlights, shadows and rouge. While Jane launched Tamara's makeover, Cara took Angie's hand and pulled her across the room to one of the windows. Cara's long brown hair hung loose past her shoulders.

"How are you doing?" Angie asked the little girl.

"Bored," she said. In case Angie didn't catch her frustration, Cara repeated, "Bored, bored, bored."

"You're not allowed to run around outside the room."

"It's like being in jail."

"Not really. This is a classy place."

These rooms were a mirror image of her suite. Designed for comfort but with a touch of luxury, the sitting room—furnished with a sofa, two overstuffed chairs and a table—was equipped with a big-screen TV, sound system and video game console as well as a kitchenette. The bedroom was in a separate chamber to the right.

With a dramatic sigh, Cara pivoted away from the window and flopped into the chair behind the desk. "Mom has a thing for one of the concierge dudes. Tomorrow, he's gonna take us out for target practice."

"I saw Waylon today." Angie had her first riding lesson, which meant she'd gotten up on the horse but hadn't gone anywhere—kind of like her undercover investigation. "He wanted me to say hello to you. As soon as everything is safe, he promises to take you out for a ride."

"Whatever." Cara rolled her eyes.

Angie recognized the attitude; this little girl had already learned not to count on promises from well-meaning adults. "Why did you want me to follow you over here? Is there something you want to tell me?"

"Look out the window."

Squinting into the darkness, Angie could see four stories down to the loading dock and a rear door from the kitchen. A couple of guys were sitting outside on the steps and talking. Across the road and to the left was the light outside the bunkhouse. The horse barn wasn't visible from this angle. "If there's something I'm supposed to see, I don't get it."

"After lunch, I was looking out and I saw her. I saw Gigi, my friend."

Her imaginary friend? "Where was she?"

"On the hill behind the bunkhouse. She dodged behind bushes. I think she's hiding from somebody, maybe the guy who punched Waylon."

A possible scenario unfolded inside Angie's head. If Gigi existed, she might have been part of a group being trafficked through this location. She might have escaped and gone into hiding at Nick's. "Can you remember the first time you played with her?"

"Exactly two weeks ago. I remember because it was a Saturday so I didn't have school. Waylon was supposed to babysit me but he was busy with the horses." She twisted a strand of hair in her fingers. "I didn't mind that he wasn't paying attention. Hanging out in the barn is cool. That's where I met Gigi. She's funny, but I think she might be a liar because she says she's nine and she's no bigger than me. She made herself a nest in one of the empty stalls."

Finding Gigi took on a new importance. The child could be in danger of being taken again by Lorenzo's men. If Angie could convince Julian to run the video from the surveillance cameras at the barn backward, they might see evidence of Cara's story. If she told him that Gigi might lead to the guy who punched Waylon, Julian might go along with her plan…or he might totally reject it. She just wasn't sure where she stood with him.

When they first met, he seemed suspicious but friendly. And when they were standing outside the horse barn under the stars, he warmed up to her, let down his guard and talked about his childhood in Wyoming. Then she pushed too hard, and Julian shut down.

He hadn't been rude over the past few days, but he kept their conversations short and to the point. He didn't seem to trust her, which was pretty much the way she felt about him. But would he help her find Cara's mysterious friend? "Have you seen Gigi again?"

"Nope."

"If you do, have your mom call me."

"Okay." Cara popped out of the chair, suddenly brimming with restless energy. "I wish you didn't have to go to that stupid party. You could stay here and play with me."

"Here's the deal," Angie said. "If you haven't seen Gigi by Monday, I'll take you with me on my riding lesson, and we'll look for her."

The kid grabbed her around the waist for a clumsy hug that really felt good. Angie stroked her fingers through the girl's smooth brown hair, and Cara snuggled against her. Their shared warmth reminded her of hugs with Marigold. Their time together on the streets of Denver had been scary but also hopeful. Marigold had been a true friend.

"We're done," Jane announced as she escorted Tamara into the room.

The makeup—including an expertly done smoky eye—was gorgeous, and Jane had used some kind of product to make Tamara's hair shine with a soft luster.

The dress was fantastic, as Angie knew it would be—bright red with a deep-V neckline and a cinched waist. "Fantastic!"

"I look good," Tamara said with a note of wonderment.

"Better than good. You look amazing, and we've got to run before Julian gets impatient and leaves without us."

Tamara gave Jane a hug and thanked her.

"No kisses," Jane said, "you'll smudge the lipstick."

"Got it," Tamara said with a giggle.

And then, they were off.

JULIAN PARKED AT the entrance to Nick's, got out of his SUV and walked around to the sidewalk. Though he wasn't usually a fan of Lorenzo's parties and did everything he could to avoid them, he had a mission tonight. Somehow, he had to snag a few minutes of private time with the boss. Lorenzo hadn't returned any of his calls or messages, and Julian needed answers about the man with the scar.

Leif Farnsworth, the former Bronco quarterback who managed the sports betting operation, sauntered over and joined him. Blond, tall and handsome, he wore a brown leather jacket tailored to fit the span of his wide shoulders. Because Leif was a jock and good-looking, many people assumed he was a slab of brainless beefcake. They were wrong.

Not only did Leif have an encyclopedic memory for sporting statistics, he could calculate percentages and odds in his head. He played violin and regularly watched performances of Opera Colorado. When he'd attended Stanford on a football scholarship, he'd actually gone to classes and learned something. Julian enjoyed spending time with him.

"Where's the rest of our carpool?" Leif asked.

"The ladies are running late. No surprise. We're going with Tamara and Angie."

"Angie's a hard worker. She's been keeping her pretty little nose to the grindstone."

"Zapata gave her a deadline."

"Got it." Leif nodded. Zapata had a reputation of being dangerous. Not even a semifamous former athlete dared to cross him. "What's the story with Angie? What makes her tick?"

"She's single, spent the last couple of years in California, hates horses and is good at hand-to-hand combat. She had Murph on his knees in two minutes."

"Dangerous and beautiful, that's a scary combination, like a Venus flytrap."

The two women came through the exit side by side. When Julian spotted Angie dressed in shimmering white and gold, his heart flip-flopped inside his rib cage, which was not the reaction he wanted. Being attracted to her would, most likely, lead to trouble.

Beside him, Leif seemed to be having heart palpitations of his own. His voice caught in his throat. "I've never seen Tamara look like this. Red is good on her."

In her vivacious dress with the neckline that plunged all the way down, Tamara Rigby transformed from the uniformed supervisor for hotel operations to a creature of passion and maybe even desire. Julian had thought for a long time that Leif and Tamara would make a good couple. Both were smart; Tamara had an MBA in hospitality management. And both were cultured. Both had talents that were wasted at Nick's. Though Julian paid them well and promoted them quickly, he knew that these two could do better.

He nudged Leif's shoulder and said, "Let's make sure she's sitting in the back with you."

As soon as the women were seated with Angie in the passenger seat beside him, Julian pulled away from the curb. He tuned the radio to a classical station that was playing Rossini's greatest hits. The couple in the back seat of the SUV chatted intelligently about lyric opera in the early 1800s and this piece—a favorite of Tamara's—from *The Barber of Seville.*

Angie peered into the rear of the SUV, listened to them and then looked at him. "You must have known that Leif and Tamara were both opera fans. I think maybe you were playing matchmaker."

"I just set up the carpool."

"And I appreciate the ride." As she reached up to smooth her already perfect hairstyle, the glow from the dashboard highlighted her delicate profile. "Did you want for us to ride together for some kind of protection, likc a safety-in-numbers thing?"

"Why would you think that?"

"After we talked to Waylon, you upped the security. Employees—especially the women—are escorted to the parking lot after dark. Cara and Jane are still living on the concierge level. While I'm on that subject, I approve of those concierge guys who have got to be former military and obviously know how to handle lethal weapons. Anyway, I'm guessing you never found the man with the scar."

He tried to brush her off. "I have the situation under control."

"Do you?"

There was an edge to her voice, and he wondered about her underlying motives. "My precautions are to make sure nobody else gets hurt. If you don't mind, let's drop it."

"Okay, but I'm still a little nervous. When you looked at the feeds from your surveillance cameras, did you find anything that might lead to the guy who attacked Waylon?"

"Not a thing."

He didn't have to repeat his request for her to drop the topic because Leif and Tamara had launched into a sing-along with the radio—a karaoke performance of the "Figaro, Figaro, Figaro" aria. If he'd told Angie about the surveillance feeds, it would have been a short conversation. He'd seen the man with the scar attack Waylon. There had been no audio to show what they were saying to each other but the video gave a clear picture of a bully attacking an old cowboy.

Over and over, Julian had studied the tapes. He'd memorized the physical characteristics of the man with the scar, learned how he walked and how he gestured with his hands. He and Gordon put together a facial recognition package that would alert them if the man with the scar showed up again at Nick's. It was important to find out what this guy was after.

The assailant had been lurking around outside the barn and the bunkhouse, which might be significant. Right now, that bunkhouse was unoccupied, but it was furnished with ten bunkbeds, a propane heater and stove. It was big enough for people to live there. Perfect for human trafficking.

As he drove through the western outskirts of Denver, his fingers tensed on the steering wheel. For the past couple of months, he'd been worrying about subtle changes in operations that would affect Nick's. He'd become aware of a cover-up. Conversations would shut down when he joined the group. His receipts had been audited by Zapata's team of accountants…twice.

After putting together bits and pieces of information, his best guess was that Nick's was about to be turned into a hub for human trafficking. He hated that idea. The victims of these operations were little more than slaves—young women used for sex, indentured day laborers, forced housekeepers and nannies. When they were first hiring at Nick's, he'd been adamant about green cards and fair wages. He'd made his opinions known, and a lot of the guys weren't happy about his strict rules governing the women who worked in the Burlesque.

Tonight, he had to talk to Lorenzo and get answers. Not knowing what to expect was killing him. The only thing worse would be to learn the ugly truth.

Chapter Seven

"We're almost there," Julian announced. "Over there, on the right, you can see the house."

From the back seat, Tamara said, "I've heard a lot about this place. People call it the Glass Palace."

Angie leaned forward in the passenger seat of Julian's SUV and peered through the night, trying to get a better look at Lorenzo's unusual mansion. The upscale neighborhood in an area southwest of Denver consisted of sprawling properties of two, three or five acres that were landscaped for privacy with a combination of conifers, cottonwoods and aspens that blended into the rocky hillsides of a national forest. In this season—early October before the first major snowfall—the aspen leaves flashed gold in Julian's headlights.

He drove the SUV into a line of cars on a long, winding, two-lane road leading to the entrance. The closer they got to the house, the more spectacular it was. Dramatic spotlights defined the sharp angles of a modernistic design. The towering front of the house was floor-to-ceiling windows. Inside, Lorenzo's guests milled throughout, talking and drinking on three different levels. There were staircases, and a transparent cylinder that housed an elevator. For sure, this was a palace. Incredible!

She reminded herself that this remarkable structure had been built with the profits of gritty, sleazy crime, which really wasn't a valid reason to find fault with the building. Instead she aimed her hostility at the residents of the house who were fair game for criticism. "You know what they say about people who live in glass houses."

From the back seat came the rumbling baritone of Leif Farnsworth. "They shouldn't throw stones."

"And they shouldn't walk around naked," said Tamara. "And they can't have secrets."

"I'm not so sure about that," Angie said. "Lorenzo has secrets."

"Everybody does," Julian said. "Tamara was commenting on the transparency of a glass house. The secrets are there, but it's hard to keep them hidden."

"I guess you're right. We all have secrets," she mused. This might be an opportunity to gather information from the others in her carpool. Not that she thought Tamara was hiding something that might pertain to her investigation. She didn't know whether Leif deserved closer scrutiny, but Julian had secrcts that had baby secrets of their own. "I've got a game for us. We go around the car, and each one of us tells a secret."

"Okay," Tamara said. "Here's mine. I was married and divorced before I was twenty-two. And it wasn't for the reason you might suspect. I wasn't pregnant… just a bad judge of character."

"I never would have guessed that you had a wild side," Leif said.

"I don't, not really. After that, I learned to be even more careful."

"Tell that to your sexy red dress," he said. "Here's my big secret. This is actually something that bothers me. I never graduated from Stanford. I'm four credits short."

Angie heard the pain in his voice, and she was glad when Tamara leaned over to console him. Those two had bonded like Velcro. She turned her focus on the man in the driver's seat. "Your turn, Julian."

"After you, I insist."

She wasn't constrained to the truth. Every trace of her real background had been erased. No one could tell if she was lying her ears off, which made her urge to share something of herself seem odd and unnecessary. For just this once, she wanted to bypass deception.

"I grew up in foster care," she said.

Honesty spilled through her lips and spread around her like a goopy puddle. Her wall of defense was melting.

"What happened to your parents?" Tamara asked.

"The system lost track of my father when I was a kid. Mom was an addict who was in and out of jail. I suppose I could find her if I wanted. But I don't."

"Was there anyone else?" Tamara said. "Any family."

"There was a girl who was my age." This was the second time she'd thought of Marigold in just a few hours. Being this close to Lorenzo must be sparking dangerous memories. "We were closer than sisters but life tore us apart. I miss her every single day."

Tears welled up behind her eyelids. *This is crazy! I don't cry.* This kind of uncensored reaction was why she avoided the truth. Sure, she had a lousy childhood and missed Marigold with all her heart, but those factors wouldn't help her solve the human trafficking issue. Her personal heartache wasn't enough to land Lorenzo in prison.

"What about Julian's secret?" Tamara asked. "Come clean, boss."

He shifted position behind the steering wheel, and Angie could tell that he was reluctant to open up. The fact that they had that defensive attitude in common made her wonder what else they shared. "Here goes," he said. "It's no secret that I'm not a drinker or a gambler, but very few people know that I'm an addict. I've been sober for six years."

"Were you in AA?" Leif asked.

"Hell, yes. I did years of group meetings and one-on-one therapy. It's not easy to restart your life…nothing about addiction is easy. Every time I hear a dealer shuffle or a roulette wheel whir I get that prickly feeling across my shoulders. The cash in my wallet is ready to play. The worst part is that I can't drown my desire to gamble in booze or pot or any other high."

"Why on earth do you work here?" Tamara asked.

Angie knew the answer. To defeat your demons you had to face them. That was the reason she had joined the FBI. She needed to study and comprehend the many ways law enforcement had failed her as a child, and then she needed to do something about it.

Julian shot her a glance. "Maybe I like to play with fire."

"I get it." She finished his thought. "Be careful that you don't get burned."

AS JULIAN GUIDED the SUV in the line of cars leading to the front entrance of Lorenzo's house, his anxiety expanded inch by inch. Talking about his addiction was hard. Old fears and frustrations raked up and churned inside him. He hadn't been to a meeting in over a year. Maybe it was time to start again.

Angie huffed. "Why are we going so slow?"

"My guess," Julian said, "is that there's a metal detector at the door, and the valets are holding the cars until they're sure the guests are clean."

Apparently, he wasn't the only person who was serious about security. Frisking a bunch of gangsters was bound to take a while. He wouldn't be subject to a search. As manager of Nick's, Julian was above suspicion. He adjusted the bulge of his shoulder holster under his jacket, confident that he wouldn't be asked to disarm. He glanced between the seats and made eye contact with Leif. "Are you carrying?"

"Not tonight."

"Ladies, how about you?"

"Oh, please," Angie said. "Weapons make lousy accessories."

Since they weren't armed and therefore wouldn't run into trouble from the guys with the metal detectors, Julian could slip the SUV out of this interminable caravan and detour around to the rear of the house. He eased onto the shoulder of the road and drove to a one-lane dirt road—a path, really—that took a couple of quick turns and disappeared into the trees.

"Where are we going?" Tamara asked.

"The service entrance in the back."

He'd visited the Glass Palace several times and had taken every opportunity to study the architecture. The central structure was built in the 1920s when Frank Lloyd Wright's clean, modern style was popular. The house had been upgraded and expanded two or three times, including the replacement of much of the glass with quadruple-pane, bulletproof sheets that maintained the appearance of transparency but were as strong as a fortress.

The SUV bounced along the unpaved path as it curled through stands of trees and massive, granite chunks. Lights from the house glittered through the forest, enticing them to come closer. The sounds of conversation and laughter mingled with an undercurrent of music from a piano.

Finally, he drove into a clearing outside the house where several other vehicles from the caterers and waiters were parked. Julian would have to jockey around to find a space to leave his SUV that wasn't in the way.

He slipped the car into Park. "You three might as well go inside. After I find parking, I'll join you."

"Are you sure you don't want company?" Angie asked. "I'll wait with you."

"Go, I'll catch up with you later."

He shooed them away, glad to have a moment of solitude before he entered Lorenzo's den and confronted him about the man with the scar. Leaning back in his seat, Julian turned off the headlights and inhaled a breath, hoping to center himself before he made his next move. From where he was sitting, he could see the kitchen area that fitted into the hillside behind the house. Toward the front, he saw three stories of glass and an acrylic staircase with steel gray steps that matched the polished marble on the floor. The people moving through this scene appeared to be floating. He noticed Angie melting into the crowd as she talked to Rudy and Carlos. Her glittering white-and-gold jumpsuit contrasted the men in dark suits. Not a surprise. No matter where she went, Angie would stand out.

His gaze was drawn to a guy in a silk shirt and a black vest who wore a baseball cap. His outfit was more casual than most of the other guests but not enough to make him too obvious. The thing that caught Julian's attention was the man's gait. As he moved across the second floor level and descended the staircase, his stride matched the figure Julian had been studying for two days on the surveillance feed from the barn. The scar on his forehead was hidden by that baseball cap and he'd shaved the beard, but the way he moved was familiar. When the guy tapped somebody else on the chest, Julian swore under his breath. He'd seen that gesture a hundred times, had memorized the shape of those stubby fingers. No doubt about it. This was the man who attacked Waylon.

Though his SUV was blocking two other cars, Julian didn't have time to search for a good parking spot. This might be his only chance to nab this guy. He threw open his car door and charged toward the house just as the man in the baseball cap stepped outside.

Trying not to alert the guy, Julian slowed his pace and ducked behind a blue delivery van from Valentino's Bakery and Wedding Cakes. When he peeked around the edge of the van, he saw the guy with the baseball cap staring directly at him.

Fine. Julian wasn't in the mood for games. He stepped into the light, no point in trying to hide. He was ready for this showdown.

The thug yanked off his cap and pushed back the hair on his forehead to show the jagged outline of his scar. His upper lip curled in a sneer, taunting. He stuck the cap back on his head and took off running, dodging through vehicles and diving into the forest.

Julian sprinted after him. While he ran, he drew his Glock from the shoulder holster. Though he couldn't see clearly enough to take aim, he needed to be ready. Slapping aside the low-hanging branches and stepping around rock formations, he went deeper into the forest.

As they got farther away from the Glass Palace, the darkness intensified. The moon was on the wane, and starlight barely penetrated the overhead branches. His pursuit was based more on instinct than vision. He stumbled and came to a stop amid a circle of rugged pine trunks.

Trying to ignore the noise from the party, Julian listened intently. He cast back in his memory to his youth in Wyoming when he'd gone hunting every weekend. In the dark, he couldn't use his ability as a tracker, not when it was important to move fast. He took off his glasses and closed his eyes. When he opened them, he saw the faint trail leading into the forest. Far ahead, he saw the leaves on a chokecherry bush rustle.

He figured the guy wouldn't go right because that direction led to the road and the endless line of cars approaching the house. Uphill to the left was the most likely direction. Did he see branches shaking? Did he hear the heavy breathing of a man on the run?

From behind, he heard someone approaching. Had the guy doubled back? Julian slipped into the shadow of a tree, raised his weapon and waited. Leif Farnsworth staggered forward.

Julian blocked his path. "What are you doing here?"

"Don't shoot. I thought I could help."

"Why are you here?"

"I dropped off the ladies, and then I went outside to find you. It didn't seem right for you to miss the party because you were parking the car." Moonlight spread across his shoulders, emphasizing a shrug. "I saw you running after a guy."

"And you jumped right in."

"Good guess, Professor. I know there's something weird going on at Nick's, something weirder than usual. If you let me, I'll help."

Julian didn't know how much he trusted the big man, but he knew Leif wasn't an idiot. He had a temper and was aware of the ethical problem of working for Lorenzo, but wasn't foolish.

Julian lowered his gun. "You go right. I'll go left. If you see him, yell."

"I'm on it."

The former quarterback darted through the trees as though evading a pass rush from the defensive line. Julian tried not to think of how Leif earned his nickname of "Falling Leif" because he'd been sacked so many times. Their chances of catching the man with the scar were minimal at best.

He had better odds talking to Lorenzo and getting him to explain what was happening. Was the man with the scar working for him? Or was he an enemy?

Chapter Eight

Insidc the Glass Palace, Angie mingled with many guests from different strata. Solid-looking politicians rubbed shoulders with cowboys, rock musicians and divas dripping with diamonds. The attendance had to be over three hundred, and she doubted that most of them had come for the stated purpose of celebrating the sixtieth birthday of Nolan Zapata. They were here to enjoy the Glass Palace and maybe to curry favor with Nick Lorenzo. People didn't seem to care that he was a criminal who was about to sink to a new low in depravity with his human trafficking operation.

With her background and the constant deceptions that were the foundation of her life, Angie couldn't claim righteous indignation. Most definitely, she didn't think she was better than anyone else. But she hated to see Lorenzo get away with his crimes.

Rudy and Carlos joined her almost as soon as she entered. Rudy's somber outfit of black suit with black shirt and tie didn't disguise the blush of excitement that colored his cheeks. If Angie had to guess, she'd say this was the first time the kid had been invited to a grown-up event. Carlos was blasé, unflappable. He snagged a champagne glass from a passing waiter and handed it to her.

"I'm not much of a drinker," she said. Her thoughts immediately went to Julian and his sobriety. Functioning in environments like this without an alcohol buffer had to be difficult. "I don't suppose one glass will hurt."

"I'd like to hear your opinion," Carlos said. "This sparkling rosé comes from a winery on the western slope that I'm considering for an investment."

"Investment?"

"I might buy the place," he said with casual ease, suggesting that the purchase of a vineyard was no big deal.

She had to revise her opinion of Carlos. When he picked her up at the motel, she'd thought he was a low-level gofer which was terrible and inaccurate stereotyping on her part. *I need to be smarter.* She should have realized that he had status when he took a seat at the table with Zapata, Valentino and Julian. Finding out more about him would be wise, starting with learning his last name.

After a sip of bubbly, she wrinkled her nose. "It tickles my tongue, and it's kind of sweet and yummy. I'd say you should go for it. All you need is a name for the label. Maybe your family name."

"Zapata? No." He shook his head. "My *familia* has a history of controversy, even though we're now farmers and businessmen, like my uncle."

She should have known, should have done more research. Carlos was related to Nolan Zapata, and their *familia* had ties to a cartel from Colombia. She definitely needed to pay more attention to Carlos—a guy who tended to fade into the woodwork. "Whatever you call your wine, I'm sure it'll be a winner."

Rudy leaned close to her ear. "Who's the chick in the red dress you came in with?"

"Tamara Rigby, the woman who runs the hotel operations."

"No way," he said. "That mousy little worker bee is the lady in red?"

"Why don't you tell her you like the dress? I'm sure she'd appreciate the compliment." And Angie wouldn't mind time alone with Carlos. She turned to him. "How long have you been working for Lorenzo?"

"Ever since I graduated from college. My uncle wanted me to be an accountant like him, but I'm into real estate and investment. Colorado is a good place to buy and sell property."

"I'm sure that's true, but I've never seen anything like this house. Tell me about it."

As he described the layout and special features, they glided across polished marble floors toward a long table where a five-tier cake from Valentino's bakery stood waiting to be cut. This dining area had an open ceiling that was three stories high. On the second level, she spotted Tamara leaning against the clear acrylic half wall on the balcony. From the way she gestured and tossed her head, Angie could see that the lady in red was enjoying herself. On the third floor above her was Nick Lorenzo, looking down like an evil gargoyle.

She pointed him out to Carlos. "What's up there?"

"An art gallery," he said. "Behind the wall of art is the private area. That's where you find the bedrooms, bathrooms and offices."

Lorenzo's office was her targeted destination. After skillful hacking on her computer, she'd studied blueprints and also learned that there was a way to approach the office without being seen on any of the surveillance cameras. She dropped a comment that might be used as an excuse if she got caught sneaking around on the third floor. "I'd love to see the art."

"Not without an invite. Lorenzo is protective of his favorite treasures."

"The house is huge. Does anybody else live here?" In her dossier for the case, Angie had learned that Lorenzo had been divorced for years but stayed close to his three adult children. "Maybe his kids?"

"They have their own houses and condos," Carlos said. "The only other person living here right now is Marion."

"A girlfriend?" Angie had very little info on Lorenzo's mistresses. The women seemed to drift into and out of his life like waves on a shore.

"She's an artist and actually acquired some of the masterpieces hanging on his upstairs walls, but I don't expect to see her around much longer. She's getting to that age, if you know what I mean."

She knew exactly what he meant. Lorenzo liked his women young. She looked up to the third floor where he'd been standing. He was gone, which meant it was time for her to get busy.

She couldn't politely detach from Carlos who directed her toward a maroon sofa where his uncle sat like a king waiting for the peasants to come forward and kiss his ring. Nolan Zapata twirled a flute of champagne between his bejeweled fingers. The only other time she'd seen him was that first casual meeting, and Angie was impressed with how well Zapata cleaned up. His thick black hair was combed back from his forehead, and he was so clean-shaven that his jaw gleamed like marble. He wore a silver brocade jacket with tuxedo trousers. Graciously, he rose to greet her.

"Congratulations on your birthday," she said.

"Thank you for the gift. I assume you're part of the group from Nick's who chipped in to buy me that trim little motorboat."

"That would be a rational assumption." She had *not* contributed. "Have you had a chance to look over my suggestions on how we can change the off-track betting operation?"

"No talk of business tonight," he said. "I'll look at your numbers on Saturday of next week as we agreed."

She knew her first ten days would be successful. With help from the forensic accounting department at the FBI, she had perfected a computer program that upped the profits. All she really had to do was install the new algorithms and let them run.

"Carlos has been showing me around," she said. "I didn't realize that you two were related. Is your whole family from Denver?"

"We come from a small town in New Mexico by the name of Ojos Caliente."

"Hot eyes," she translated.

He lowered himself onto the sofa and patted the space beside him, indicating that she should sit. His hard-edged gaze sliced through her like a blade. "I heard you were taking riding lessons from Waylon," he said.

"I thought learning about horses would help me with the off-track betting. I'm not really fond of barnyard animals."

"Racehorses aren't like the old gray mare in the barn," he said. "Those animals are Thoroughbreds, worth more than most people."

Spoken like a man who was about to embark on a human trafficking scheme. She suspected Zapata knew all about the attack on Waylon, and she carefully eased into the topic. "Poor Waylon got into a scuffle the other day,"

"Who was he fighting with?"

"I have no idea." She lied easily. "Julian said he'd take care of it."

"And I'm sure he will," Zapata said.

Digging for information, she asked, "How many of the employees at Nick's report to you?"

"A few." He brushed off her question.

"What about security men and women?"

"Excuse me, Angie."

Abruptly, he stood, which indicated that their conversation was over. Uncle Nolan wasn't anywhere near as chatty as Carlos. She'd only known him for a few days but was fairly sure that she had the rough outline of his profile figured out. Zapata wasn't a friendly boss, beloved by his employees. More like a stern, angry father, he laid down ironclad rules and meted out harsh punishment for failure. Her best bet was to keep her distance and stay on his good side.

She worked her way across the first floor toward the staircase. On the second floor, she saw that Leif Farnsworth had joined Tamara. The gang of adoring Bronco fans who always seemed to be following him were getting in the way of his conversation with the lady in red.

Angie ascended a staircase that followed a twisting acrylic path similar to the disappearing stairs in an Escher lithograph. With all this glass and plastic, she felt like she was wandering in circles. On the third floor where she'd seen Lorenzo looking down, there were fewer people. To her right, she saw the artwork. To her left, there was a subtle door that blended into the decor. She knew that plain entrance would lead to the bedrooms and offices.

Though she could have used her ornate hair decoration to pick the locks, she'd rather not if it wasn't necessary. It wasn't. The handle turned easily in her grasp, and she slipped inside a well-lit corridor with doors on either side. According to her blueprints, there weren't supposed to be surveillance cameras down this hallway, but she didn't want to take unnecessary risks. As long as she didn't break into a room, she could claim that she'd been looking for a bathroom.

At the end of the hallway, the door was opened a crack. Angie pushed the door with her shoulder and entered an opulent bedroom. This might be a good time to back out, but she'd come this far. She saw a small desk with a laptop that might be Lorenzo's private computer.

The information she needed might be on that very hard drive…or not.

Angie cleared her throat. "Hello? Is anybody here?"

She heard a rustling on the far side of the room. A floor-to-ceiling window slid open and a woman stepped inside. As she stared at Angie, she didn't seem frightened, merely curious.

"I knew it," she said. "I knew someday we'd be back together."

"Marigold. It's you."

In that moment, everything changed.

JULIAN CREPT DOWN the hallway to the bedroom at the end. He hadn't intended to spy on Angie, but he was curious about why she moved through the crowd at the party, avoiding conversation and ignoring the lavish buffet. Her attention focused on the staircase leading to the third floor. When she ducked into the door to the private quarters, he followed. Finally, he might be able to figure out what kind of game she was playing.

From the first time he gazed into her dark, beautiful eyes, he'd suspected that she had some kind of secret agenda. With all her criminal connections and computer training, she might be part of an extortion or money laundering scheme. He doubted that she knew about the possibility of human trafficking; smuggling and transportation weren't in her wheelhouse. When she entered Lorenzo's bedroom, he moved close to the door so he could overhear what Angie was saying. The other woman in the room had to be Marion, Lorenzo's long-term mistress. No matter how many others came and went, Lorenzo kept contact with her. Marion was special to him.

Why did the two women keep saying "Marigold"? One of them was crying.

From behind his back, he heard the door to the corridor click and open. He pivoted and saw Lorenzo. The boss wasn't going to be happy about having Angie break into his private quarters. She could get fired…or worse. Julian had a better chance of survival. He was also annoyed by the way Lorenzo had ignored his calls and texts.

Before Lorenzo could speak, Julian confronted him. "I've been trying to get in touch with you for the past couple of days."

"Congratulations," Lorenzo said with an expansive gesture that displayed the tailored cut of his burgundy jacket. "You've caught up with me."

"Waylon was assaulted. I reviewed the feed from the surveillance cameras and saw his attacker sneaking around outside the barn, the garage and the bunkhouse."

"So what?" Lorenzo dusted his manicured hands as through he was disposing of the problem. "Waylon must have gotten protective about the barn and tried to chase the intruder away. The old cowboy isn't as tough as he used to be."

"I'd tend to agree with you." It was never smart to directly contradict the boss. "I'd almost decided this was nothing to worry about, but then I saw the guy here at your house, mingling with your guests as though he had every right to be here."

Lorenzo's eyes narrowed. He didn't like what he'd heard. "You're mistaken."

"Not likely. This guy has a distinctive scar on his forehead. When I approached him, he took off running."

"Did he get away from you?"

"He went into the national forest." The slimeball had planned his escape from the start. After crashing through the trees, Julian and Leif had discovered a stack of branches that had probably been used to hide a dirt bike or an ATV. There were also tire tracks. The final touch was the baseball cap he'd been wearing. Julian took the cap with a Nick's Burlesque logo from his pocket. "He left this behind."

Lorenzo snatched the cap, stared at the logo and threw it on the floor. "Son of a bitch."

"The guy is bad news," Julian said. "The way I figure, he's working for you or working for your enemies."

"He was so stupid that he got picked up by the cameras. Then he called attention to himself by getting into a brawl. How can this jackass be working for me?" Agitated, he raked his fingers through his silver hair. "I don't recognize him."

It had long been Julian's opinion that Lorenzo wasn't an effective manager. His success was based on two factors. Number one: he had a nose for sniffing out talented employees and didn't mind paying them what they were worth. Number two: he frequently came up with decent ideas for improvements.

However, when it came to the day-to-day grind of running the operation, Lorenzo checked out. As soon as he'd put Julian in charge of Nick's, he'd stepped aside.

If he was, in fact, starting up a human trafficking operation, Lorenzo would pass the major responsibility to somebody else, probably Zapata.

"He might be a new employee," Julian said. "You can't be expected to know everybody who works for you."

"True." Lorenzo paced down the corridor and back. "I'll talk to Nolan. He keeps track of new hires."

"Is there some new project you're working on?"

"Don't worry about it, Professor."

Julian pressed his point. "The guy with the scar was creeping around by the barn. Anything going on out there? Was he looking for something?"

"Hell if I know."

Julian shifted gears. "He also threatened one of the performers at the Burlesque."

"Which one?"

"Calamity Jane."

"The cowgirl with the whips and knives?" He barked a laugh. "She can handle a threat."

"If there's a new project at Nick's, I need to know." Changing direction again, Julian used an aggressive tone. "You've got to tell me so I can be prepared."

They faced off. Julian wasn't going to back down. If Lorenzo was going to jump into the dark, cruel world of trafficking and slavery, Julian couldn't stand by and let it happen. There were steps to be taken.

"Next week," Lorenzo said. "Zapata will fill you in."

Or kick me out.

The bedroom door swept open and Marion stepped through. Her ice-blue outfit sparkled with crystals, and her wavy blond hair cascaded down her back. She gave Lorenzo a peck on the cheek and then wiped off the imprint of her lipstick.

"Nice to see you, Julian." She smiled at him then turned back to Lorenzo. "We need to get downstairs. It's time to cut the cake."

"They can wait." His arm snaked around her waist, and he pulled her close against him.

"But it's time. I don't want Zapata to feel like we're disrespecting him on his birthday. He might get hungry and bite my head off."

"We can't let that happen," Lorenzo said. "By the way, Julian, nice job on the motorboat birthday present."

"Thank you, sir."

Julian followed them down the corridor. With every step, he tried to think of a reason to go into the bedroom and check on Angie. Leaving her here alone worried him. Not only did he want to be sure she got away safely but he was also curious about her connection.

At the door leaving the corridor, the lovely Marion turned to him. "I've forgotten my phone. Would you go back to the bedroom and get it for me?"

"Of course."

"Thanks so much. We'll see you downstairs."

She'd given him an excuse to check on Angic, and Julian grabbed the opportunity with both hands. He rushed into the bedroom, looked around, checked the walk-in closet and peeked into the attached bathroom. Angie was nowhere in sight.

He knew the blueprints for this house. There were no other exits from the bedroom…but there was a balcony. He opened the sliding glass door and stepped outside into a cool evening breeze. Angie crouched on the floor beside the acrylic wall that stretched the length of the balcony. Her face was buried in her hands. Her shoulders trembled with silent sobs.

Chapter Nine

Julian gathered Angie in his arms and held her while she wept. Though she barely made a sound, her body shuddered in violent bursts. Her breath hissed through clenched teeth. Whatever happened between her and Marion had shredded Angie's composure. He wanted to let her cry until she ran out of tears, but they needed to hurry and get the hell away from here. Half the people downstairs were criminals, and most of them worked for Lorenzo. All the boss had to do was give the word to make her disappear.

He stroked her shoulder under the gold jacket. "You need to calm down, please calm down. It's important for us to get to the car."

"I can't." She swabbed at her eyes with the back of her hand, smearing her eye makeup. Pieces of hair had come loose from her topknot and twisted around her face in messy disarray. "Just leave me alone."

"You can't stay here."

"And I can't go back to the damn party." With both hands, she shoved against his chest, creating space between them. Grasping one of the sleek chairs on the balcony, she dragged herself away from him. When she tried to stand, her legs crumpled and her shoulders drooped. "I look awful. It'll take forever to repair my face. People will notice."

"I have another idea." He stood. "Take off your shoes."

Too upset to question or complain, she did as he said. "Now what?"

"I've studied every inch of the blueprints for this house."

"Why?"

"The design and the architecture are fascinating. Anyway, I know this place better than Lorenzo, better than almost anybody." He took her hand, shocked by how cold she was. Her fingers felt like ice. He pulled her to her feet. "First, you're going to borrow a pair of Marion's sneakers. Then we're going to go down the fire escape."

"Are you joking?"

"It was installed in the 1950s as a safety feature," he said, "accessible only from the roof where there are no surveillance cameras."

"Well, why not?" Shaking her head, she stumbled toward the closet. "With all the amazing stuff in this house, I wouldn't be surprised if you told me we were going to fly into the forest on a magic carpet."

If Aladdin's technology had been available, Lorenzo would have bought it. Julian grabbed Marion's phone and slipped it into his jacket pocket. "Let's go. Shoes first, then we're out the door."

"We've always worn the same size. Since we were twelve, long before we ran away."

"What do you mean?"

"Nothing." She tucked her feet into a pair of black-and-white Converse high-tops from a wall of shoes in the walk-in closet.

He led her from the bedroom. At the far end of the corridor, he opened the door to a short hallway. They hurried past boxes stored on shelves and went up a flight of stairs. He paused at a metal door and looked down at her. Her makeup was a mess and her platinum hair looked like a bird's nest. He saw her innocence and her vulnerability. "Before we go outside, I need to know that you won't fall apart. Once this door closes, it's locked. We can't go back."

She lifted her chin. "I can do it."

He had to believe her. Finding another escape route was risky, and he didn't want to slip up and attract attention.

The door to the roof was stuck—probably hadn't been used in years—and he had to use his shoulder to get it open. Early October was chilly in the mountains. He took off his jacket and helped her put it on before guiding her across the roof to a ladder that hung over the edge of the parapet.

The front of the house and most of the right side were glass, but these back walls revealed a more utilitarian purpose. The fire escape from the roof was painted light brown. Otherwise, it was similar to something that might be found on an apartment building in Brooklyn.

He stepped over the edge and held on to the railing. "I forgot to ask if you're afraid of heights."

"Too late now." A weak smile flickered across her lips.

"I'll go first. If you need to stop, just let me know."

He descended backward, watching her move down the fire escape. The wind rattled around them, but the metal fire escape held firm. There were no direct lights in this area, but the glow from the rest of the house lit the trees and rocks in the forest. The farther they went, the stronger she seemed. By the time they reached the last step and he lowered the ladder, she had recovered much of her strength.

When her foot in the Converse sneaker touched the earth, he felt a whoosh of relief. They just might pull this off. "Here's the good part. We're closer to where I parked the car."

"I'm sorry I fell apart," she said with a nod. "I almost never cry. It's not like me."

"It's okay. I won't let you get hurt, I promise."

He led her around the back of the house, passing the kitchen and heading to the place where he'd parked. Fortunately, no one had pulled in behind his silver SUV and blocked the exit. They could be out of here in minutes.

First, he put through a phone call to Leif asking him to meet at the door where he'd originally dropped him off. When the former Bronco appeared, Julian handed over Marion's phone. "Make sure she gets it right away."

"Where are you headed?"

"Angie's sick. I'm taking her back to Nick's. Can you get a ride?"

"You bet, and I'll be real happy to take care of Tamara."

He drove to the front of the house and exited on the long driveway. As the SUV put miles between them and the Glass Palace, his tension ratcheted down. Not that he was relaxed, far from it.

"I have some questions," he said. "You had to be eavesdropping on what I said to Lorenzo. How much did you hear?"

"Some," she admitted. "You said something about chasing the man with the scar into the forest. Are you sure it was him?"

"I've been watching him on tape for the past couple of days. When I saw him in the house, he was taunting me, peeking out from under the cap before he made his run to a dirt bike he'd hidden behind a stack of branches. Leif joined me."

Leif's unexpected appearance seemed too convenient, maybe even suspicious, but Julian wasn't about to discuss his feelings with Angie. She owed him multiple explanations. "Another question," he said, "Why did you go to the third floor private quarters?"

"To see the artwork," she said.

That was a lie and not a very believable one. She'd been on the opposite side of the art display inside Lorenzo's bedroom. There must have been something else she went looking for. "Who's Marigold?"

"I don't know what you're talking about."

Another obvious fib? She was really off her game, and he wasn't about to waste time digging through layers of deception. "Might as well tell me."

"Or what's going to happen?"

"I'm not going to threaten you."

"Good, because we both know that never works."

"I want to help you," he said. "Just trust me. Who is Marigold?"

"Someone I never thought I'd see again." She stared through the windshield, concentrating intently on a vision he couldn't see. Was she examining her own past? "I don't like to talk about what happened to me when I was growing up. Too much sadness. Too many people who failed me. For me, foster care was horrible, but it's not like that for everybody. I was a behavior problem."

Not a surprise. "Earlier tonight, you opened up."

"Which is not like me," she said. "Usually, if somebody asks about my past, I'll make up something about winning a surfing contest in Hawaii or stealing a Van Gogh from a heartless billionaire."

"You'll lie," he said.

"It's easier, and people tend to believe me."

"You're a good liar."

"Damn right, but not tonight. When we were all telling secrets, I talked about a girl who was my closest friend. We were in the same foster homes, starting when we were twelve. We ran away from a foster home in Utah together and came to Denver. Our first job was at a strip joint."

"What else?"

"I was fifteen, and she was almost seventeen but looked younger than me, except for her breasts. She developed early. Her name was Marigold."

Julian's pause was just a second too long, but she

noticed. "Don't feel sorry for me. My mistakes when I was with Marigold were motivation for turning my life around."

A picture began to form inside his head. "You said you'd lost touch with her."

"She was taken away from me. The guy who ran the strip joint took her and a couple of others to a private party. I'm guessing the event was similar to the one we just attended with a lot of booze and shiny surfaces to hide the decadence."

"Decadent? Zapata's birthday party seemed innocent."

"Now who's lying?" she scoffed. "We both know that the real excitement doesn't start until after midnight. That's when they bring in the pretty girls to dress the place up."

Julian didn't usually stick around for the late-night lap dances. Being sober brought out the ugliness. "Your friend Marigold was selected but not you. Why not?"

"I wasn't a party girl. I was a gawky fifteen-year-old, flat-chested with dull brown hair and scraggly teeth in need of braces. I didn't know how to dress, didn't know how to put on makeup. I wasn't pretty." She lifted her chin and looked down her nose. "Make no mistake, Julian. It takes a lot of effort to look the way I usually do."

"What happened to Marigold?"

"She hooked up with the big boss, and I bet you already know that his name was Nick Lorenzo. Marigold came back to me a couple of times and showed me jewelry he bought for her. She thought it was love, that he was her prince. I couldn't blame her for turning her back on me."

"She wasn't eighteen," he said. "It was rape."

"That was what I tried to tell the cops. All that got me was a big, fat nothing. I got shipped back to the foster home in Utah."

The pieces of her story were falling into place. His instincts about her were correct; she had underlying motives. Starting a new job with Lorenzo was only part of the reason she'd come to Colorado. Needing to give her his full attention, he took advantage of the solitude on this curving mountain road by driving onto a wide space on the shoulder and turning off the headlights. As night settled around them, he turned to her.

"Let me see if I've got this right," he said. "Marigold is the real reason you took this job. You wanted to find out what had happened to her."

"I need to know. Marigold was my dearest friend, and she vanished without a trace. It was like her existence had been erased. I did a ton of computer research and even came to Denver twice to look for her. Nothing!"

"And you thought if you infiltrated Lorenzo's organization, you'd figure it out."

"Do you know what it's like?" she asked. "To lose someone you love hurts, but to never know what happened to them makes it worse."

Threads of anger wove through her voice. Having already spent the tears and sadness of grief, she'd moved on to rage. Her tangled hair and smeared makeup gave him a hint of the gawky teenager she once had been—

the young woman who had been abandoned by Marigold. Gently, he held her hand and waited until she was ready to continue.

"I blamed Lorenzo," she said, "and I hated him. I thought he'd funneled Marigold into some kind of trafficking operation, turning her into a high-priced escort or a sex slave. I even thought he might have had her killed."

"What was your plan tonight? Did you go to the third floor to confront him?"

"That's a hard no. Guys like him never confess."

"Why were you there?"

"Investigating," she said. "I'd done a computer search of my own, looking for Marigold, but I thought I might learn something different if I could download the hard drive from Lorenzo's personal computer."

"A long shot," he said.

"And I didn't follow through. I saw his laptop but didn't snatch it."

"Why not?"

"I never expected to walk through that door and see her standing there." Angie's fingers twisted in his grasp as though her hands had a life of their own. "When we were kids...she chose to stay with him. She wanted that life."

"And now?"

"She says she's ready to leave Lorenzo, and I've got to believe her. Marigold is done with him. She promised to meet with me on Monday night. Then we'll figure out what to do."

He knew that her escape wasn't a simple matter of

walking away. In her role as Lorenzo's mistress, Marigold had been privy to the inner workings of the organization. "She's been with him for eleven years."

"I know." Angie nodded sadly. "Think of everything she's witnessed. Her testimony could probably put Lorenzo, Zapata and a dozen other guys in prison."

He hated the idea of Angie meeting with this woman. "Marigold isn't the teenager you remember. How do you know you can trust her?"

"I don't."

"It might be smart for you to step aside and leave it to the cops to rescue her. The only way she can be safe is if she's a protected witness."

"She'll never go for that." Angie wrung her hands. "Protective custody is just another type of prison. She needs to be free."

He suspected Angie was correct. His acquaintance with the woman who had been with Lorenzo for years and went by the name of Marion was limited, but she didn't strike him as someone who would quietly fade away. She was trouble, and he wouldn't let that danger spill onto Angie. She deserved better.

Chapter Ten

A little more than twenty-four hours later, it was close to midnight, and Angie had recovered. She'd showered, slept for a full ten hours, gotten dressed, splashed on a coat of bright red lipstick and come up with a plan of action. Not only would she free Marigold from Lorenzo's slimy tentacles but would also complete her undercover mission of shutting down a human trafficking ring. *That's right, I'm a superstar!* Angie liked the symmetry of linking Marigold, who had once been the victim of a predator, to saving countless other women from a similar fate at the hands of traffickers.

Dressed in a dark leather jacket with a knit cap covering her shiny platinum ponytail, she crept toward the parking area near the loading dock behind Nick's where she knew a blue delivery van from Valentino's Bakery and Wedding Cakes was parked. She'd been watching from the window of her suite and had seen Valentino leave his van, which was when she put her plan in gear. Hidden in shadow, she flattened her back against the wood siding and peered through the night, trying to calculate the angles she'd have to follow to avoid being seen on the surveillance cameras. Her intended strategy had been to fasten a tracking device onto the van, but that wouldn't be possible. She couldn't tiptoe across the space without being spotted on camera.

The alternative was old-school; she'd have to tail his van in her car. Following the sidewalk around the building, she picked up her hatchback from the lot and drove to a position where she could follow Valentino when he left. Finally, her investigation was making progress… or was it?

After seeing Marigold, Angie had gone through more mood swings than an aerialist on a flying trapeze which was a particularly apt comparison because she, too, was working without a net. Of course, she was happy, elated, delighted to find her friend. But she couldn't forget the pain when she'd been abandoned. Her thoughts ranged from a deep-rooted desire to call for help from an FBI task force to the extreme opposite—forgetting she'd ever seen Marigold. Why should Angie risk her life and her career for a woman who had chosen to stay with Lorenzo and had made zero effort to contact her for eleven years? Marigold didn't deserve her friendship or her loyalty.

Slouched in the dark behind her steering wheel, Angie closed her eyes. Memories swarmed through her mind. She thought of their adventures when they'd hitchhiked across the Rockies and worked for a few days on a river raft on the Roaring Fork. In Denver, they'd done a bit of juggling on the street as buskers. Most of all, she remembered the warmth of having somebody who loved her no matter what.

She opened her eyes. Today, she'd come to the conclusion that the best way to help Marigold was to fulfill her undercover mission and expose the trafficking operation. Who was being taken? How were they being used? Where were they dropped? Obviously, money was involved, a lot of money, which led her to the conclusion that Zapata was the mastermind, using his position in the Lorenzo organization and negotiating with his cartel connections. In her gut, she knew he was the evil genius, but she didn't have evidence to obtain warrants and didn't know when the full-scale operation would start. She suspected trial runs were already underway.

Oddly, it was Julian who pointed her toward investigating. Since last night, he'd been hovering around her, watching for signs of mental collapse. When he took her to lunch in the coffee shop, she felt his electric blue gaze sliding over her like some kind of cool, sexy, mysterious caress. *Not the way I want to think about him!* Julian was smart and incredibly good-looking, but he was also a crook and would be swept into the same net as the others when arrests were made. She needed to be more guarded around him. Last night, she might have let something slip that made him think she was a cop.

At lunch, he couldn't stop talking about the man with the scar. Julian was obsessed and worried that this guy was part of a larger operation. *Like human trafficking?* She poked around the edges of that scheme, but he wasn't thinking that way. He sensed that she was in danger and wanted her to quit working at the OTB and go home to California. As if he could protect her? The idea made her laugh. As a trained FBI operative, she shouldn't require help from him or anybody else for that matter.

As she waited for the van, she checked her phone and saw a text from Julian. Not surprising that he wouldn't call at eleven thirty on a Sunday night. It was much too late. She read his message: Surveillance cameras pay off. I have facial recog on man with scar. He's in the casino. This may be over soon.

Though tempted to call him back and join his investigation, she decided to stick with Valentino. Earlier today, she'd overheard him telling Zapata that the fleet of delivery vans belonged to him, and he gave the orders. A disagreement between these two powerful men might lead to evidence that she could use. After a bit of computer research, she learned that Valentino had eleven vans and operated bakeries in five different locations, including Colorado Springs. His business seemed tailor-made as a cover for smuggling people throughout the state.

Though she wasn't an expert when it came to collecting forensic evidence, she hoped to find a clue in his vans—fibers, fingerprints, a discarded tissue, an article of clothing or a toy. She hated that children were part of trafficking, and she still hadn't forgotten her promise to Cara. Tomorrow, they'd search for Gigi in the hills behind the bunkhouse. Tomorrow night, she'd meet with Marigold.

The dark blue van drove past the spot where she was parked. The game was on!

Angie waited until the van was almost out of sight before following. Near midnight on a Sunday, the traffic on these mountain roads was almost nonexistent so she didn't need to worry about blending. Her challenge was to keep him from noticing that she was behind him.

Living in Southern California for years, she'd spent hours every day in a car, had learned how to maneuver through eight-lane highways and had developed skills in pulling 180-degree turns, sudden stops and reversing directions. Car chases and vehicular pursuit were pretty much her kind of thing. She kept her distance on the curving mountain roads. There was really only one route that went directly into Denver. Occasionally, she'd speed up to make sure the van was still on the same road, and then she'd drop back.

When they got to the outskirts of Denver, there was more traffic. From the direction the van was traveling, she figured that Valentino was headed toward his bakery in a southwest Denver suburb—a location she'd looked up online and programmed into her GPS.

She exited a main road and drove south two blocks to the small strip mall with the bakery. A half block away from the mall, she parked and killed the headlights. At this hour, all the shops were closed and locked. Outdoor lights shone on the asphalt parking outside the dry cleaner, electronics store, hair salon and a couple of others. Valentino's Bakery and Wedding Cakes was on the end. She saw him drive around to the back. *Time to make her move.* Since she didn't know how long he'd be at the shop, she hustled. There was no need to bother with being stealthy. No witnesses were on the street, not even a late-night walker with a dog.

She tried the handle on the van. It was locked. This

utilitarian vehicle didn't have a fancy security system, and she was confident that she could break in. While she was digging in her small purse, the back door from the bakery slammed open.

"Who's out there?" Valentino bellowed.

Silhouetted by light from inside the bakery, Valentino took up nearly the entire doorway. His height wasn't much above average, but his extra-wide girth showed the result of consuming too many cakes, cookies and fresh baked breads. Not that he was soft. He had the shoulders of a Brahman bull and looked like he could lift a delivery truck.

Though she had a friendly relationship with him, she was in serious danger. Valentino had a reputation for violence. His nickname—the Baker—came from an incident when he crammed one of his enemies into an oven and set the temperature to 400 degrees. He glared at her with tired, red-rimmed eyes. In his right hand, he brandished a heavy marble rolling pin.

Her instinct was to run, but he'd already seen her. Even if she managed to escape, he knew where she lived and could bring down the wrath of Lorenzo upon her. As always, she was prepared to protect herself. There hadn't been time to subtly hide her weapons before she took off to follow his van, so she'd slipped her snub-nosed Beretta Tomcat into the small plaid purse she wore on a strap across her chest. She placed her hand on the purse's flap, ready to draw if necessary. In spite of his legendary temper, she didn't want to shoot the man. Valentino had a wife and four children.

Angie straightened her shoulders and confronted him. "We need to talk."

"How the hell did you find me?"

"I followed your truck from Nick's. I thought about tooting my horn and getting you to pull over. And I tried to signal you while we were driving."

He smacked the rolling pin against his left palm. "It's late. What the hell do you want?"

"Please don't be angry." Hoping to defuse his hostility, she played to his ego. "I need your advice. You're smart. You know how this organization runs."

"Go on."

"Over the past couple of days, I proved to Zapata that I could boost the profit margin for OTB, but he's going to fire me unless I do better." She amped up her appeal by snatching the knit cap off her head and letting her long, platinum ponytail swing free, which was usually an effective distraction. "I have an idea that I want to run by you."

"You got two minutes." When he leaned toward her, his scowling face—with downturned mouth and heavy, black eyebrows—seemed as big and round as a full, angry moon. "Talk."

"I was in my suite, looking out my window, and I saw your truck, and I thought of...cake. Not just any cake, oh, no, but a spectacular cake with a track and horse racing decorations. I wanted to tell you, and I ran downstairs to find you. But you were already driving away. So I hopped in my car and followed."

He nodded, apparently believing her lame explanation. "Tell me about the cake."

"I want to host a reception for all the members who placed bets with OTB this year." Thinking fast, she was creating this plan on the fly. Actually, an exclusive party wasn't a bad way to promote more gambling, which meant more losses and more income. "Can I come inside and talk about it?"

Now that he seemed appeased and unlikely to kill her, she wanted to press her advantage and check out the interior of the bakery. Though Valentino's name was emblazoned across the front and customers visited during the day, this location might be a good stopping point for trafficking. The area behind the shops was hidden by a tall fence and shrubs, and the street in front had very little traffic.

"You're full of crap," he said.

"So I've been told."

"But as long as you're here..." He pushed the door open and stepped aside. "Talk fast. I only stopped by to pick up some paperwork and leave notes for the morning crew. Then I go home and sleep till noon."

Inside the large kitchen, the stainless steel ovens, refrigerators, mixing vats and cooling racks gleamed under bright lighting. The delicious aromas of sugar, chocolate and baking dough scented the air. The countertops, worktables and chopping blocks were clean and organized. Everything was spick-and-span as befitted a professional bakery, which wasn't a surprise to her. Every time she'd tasted his wares, she'd been impressed by the luscious, rich quality. The Baker was a pro when it came to his craft, but that didn't mean he was a decent human being.

She kept a wary gaze on Valentino while meandering toward the open doorway that led to the customer entrance and the display cases at the front of the shop. Though she was fairly certain that the delivery trucks were being used to transport illegal cargo, this shop probably wasn't a destination. There wasn't enough extra space to hide much of anything, and the strip mall probably rested on a concrete slab with no basement. "So this is where the magic happens."

"Magic?"

"I've had your cakes. You are a magician."

He didn't smile or preen at her compliment, but he did set aside his marble rolling pin, which she considered to be progress. "This shop is mostly for doughnuts and breakfast goods. My wife thinks I should add tables so people can sit and have a meal, but that's not for me."

"I understand. You're a baker, not a chef."

"Exactly, and I've got dozens of regular outlets for my product all over town. My trucks are running all day." He lumbered to a cubicle office with glass walls on the upper half and started shuffling through paperwork. Unlike the pristine area dedicated to baking, the office was cluttered. "This big party of yours, did you run it past your boyfriend?"

"Boyfriend?"

"Come on, Angie. You know who I'm talking about. Half the strippers at Nick's are heartbroken that Julian has the hots for you."

Cara would have wanted her to remind him that the women working at the Burlesque were performers not strippers, but Angie didn't want to offend the Baker. She moved closer to his glass office. Learning his schedule would be useful. He might keep notes on where his delivery trucks were supposed to make pickups and drop-offs. "I'm still thinking about the timing for my party. Could we do it week after next?"

"That's close to Halloween. We usually have special cakes for parties and sugar skulls for Dia de los Muertos. But I can try to fit you in."

She sidled around the glass wall and entered his office. "Maybe I could take a look at your calendar."

"Don't crowd me."

A rattling noise, like a door handle being shaken, came from the front of the store. She took a backward step and craned her neck to look in that direction. "What was that?"

In the few seconds it took for her to turn back toward the Baker, he'd whipped open a file cabinet beside his desk and taken out a semiautomatic AK-47 that made her Tomcat look like a kid's toy. The barrel of the gun aimed at her gut. *No, no, no, no...* "What are you doing?"

"Somebody's at the front," the Baker said. "If it's a friend of yours, you'll be sorry."

"I don't know who it is, I swear." Moving fast, she backpedaled across the kitchen, avoiding the stainless steel tables and cabinets. Should she take the gun from her purse? She was afraid he'd see it as a threat, and she didn't want him to retaliate. "I'm on your side."

The rattle became the crash of glass shattering. The front of the store was dark, and she couldn't see anything. On the side of the kitchen opposite Valentino's office, she ducked under a table. The Baker hid behind a refrigerator.

When she saw the man who swaggered through the door and entered the kitchen, she gasped. He had stubble and a scar across his forehead. It had to be the guy Julian was searching for. Why was he here? What did he want? Julian was supposed to be watching him at the casino. His semiautomatic weapon was a match for the one Valentino held. She could tell that he wasn't alone.

The man with the scar gave the orders. "Show yourself, Baker."

"I got nothing to say to you."

"Zapata isn't happy. He doesn't think you can handle more responsibility."

"He should tell me himself, and you should get the hell out of my bakery."

"Are you threatening me, Baker?"

"That's right, Damien."

Damien worked for Zapata. As soon as she got clear of this situation, she could use that information. A thug like Damien had to be wanted by the FBI, which meant she could call on their resources to pick him up without compromising her investigation.

She ducked lower and froze in place. Damien hadn't noticed her. He kept his attention focused in Valentino's direction as he took a few tentative steps into the kitchen with his weapon at the ready.

"You made a mistake," Damien said. "Your men let that little girl get away. She could cause all kinds of trouble."

A girl who escaped? Gigi?

"Not my men," Valentino roared. "Your guys messed up. They were so busy jabbering at each other that they lost track of what was going on with her."

"Not a chance. My men are pros." He moved closer. "There's no need for us to have a problem. Put your hands up and come with me. I don't have to hurt you, Baker."

She didn't believe him.

Neither did Valentino.

The Baker stepped out from behind the fridge and sprayed bullets at Damien, who managed to get off a blast of his own before he fell. His blood splattered the appliances and stained the spotless, tiled floor. Angie pulled her Beretta Tomcat from her tiny purse. She'd gone through weapons training at Quantico but had never killed anyone.

A second man dove through the door. He dodged across the floor in a frantic dance and ducked behind a giant mixing vat. He raised his weapon, but Valentino fired first, and the second man went down.

Angie watched the one-sided battle with a terrible combination of fear and awe. Her pulse raced. She wanted to move but didn't know where to go. A third man slipped through the door into the kitchen. In a crouch, he ran between the mixing tables, coming in her direction. Neither of the other men had taken any notice of her, but he seemed to sense her presence. He was too damn close.

She braced her elbows on the stainless steel table to steady her aim. Her weapon fired one shot at a time, and she couldn't afford to lose a single bullet.

The third man squinted as if actually seeing her for the first time. He swung his semiautomatic in her direction. She should shoot now. *Now!* If he got off the first volley, she'd be dead before she had a chance to return fire. She didn't want to kill him. A dead man couldn't give her any information. Aiming at his shoulder, she squeezed the trigger.

He took her bullet without falling down. Her shot was inconsequential. He barely slowed his pace as he continued to come at her. On the other side of the kitchen, she saw the Baker take advantage of the momentary distraction caused by her shot. He blasted the third man.

She sank to the floor, gasping for breath and trembling. When she looked down, she saw that the sleeves of her jacket were speckled with the third man's blood.

Three were dead,

There were no more.

Chapter Eleven

There was movement from the front of the shop and the sound of someone kicking through the broken glass from the window. A voice called out, "Hold your fire. It's me, Julian Parisi. Are you all right?"

The Baker aimed his weapon at the open doorway. "Are these bastards with you?"

"You know they aren't." His voice was angry. "I overheard you yelling at each other. You knew that Damien worked for Zapata. I've been chasing all over the damn place, looking for him. All the while, you knew I was wasting my time. You knew who he was."

"Maybe you're not so smart, Professor."

This was only the second time she'd heard anyone use Julian's nickname, and she didn't miss the sneer in Valentino's tone. In spite of Julian's intelligence, he didn't have much in the way of street smarts.

"Here's my question," the Baker said. "If you weren't working with Damien, how did you end up here in the middle of the night?"

"I saw him at Nick's, picked him up with facial recognition on the surveillance cameras. Instead of grabbing him, I followed him when he left the casino and got in his car. I didn't know he was coming here, didn't know he was gunning for you."

The Baker heaved a heavy sigh. "You got anybody else with you?"

"Rudy and two other guys," Julian said. "Are we done talking? I need to get in there and clean up your mess before the cops arrive."

"Yeah, you can come in."

He stepped through the door with his hands raised over his head, which was smart because Valentino was still armed and ready to shoot anybody who irritated him. When Julian looked in her direction, she could tell he was surprised to see her and angry, very angry. "Good evening, Angie."

The sound of his voice comforted and disturbed her at the same time. Even though he'd given an explanation for why he was here, the timing of his arrival felt strangely coincidental. Not that she thought he was working with the cartel like Zapata, but she knew that Julian was an important cog in Lorenzo's machine.

She looked from the dead men on the floor to Julian. Both sides of this battle were criminals. There was nobody to root for. She tried to force a smile but failed. "Glad to see you."

He turned his back on her and asked the Baker, "What's she doing here?"

"Buying a cake."

"At midnight on a Sunday?" He shook his head in disgust and disbelief. "That's what I call a half-baked story."

Valentino chuckled. "Good one."

Julian leaned over Damien's body, felt for a pulse and shot her a glance. "Did you kill him, Angie?"

"She tried." The Baker illustrated by making his thumb and forefinger into a gun. "Blondie has a little pop gun in her purse."

How could he make jokes? She stared into the lifeless eyes of the man who had fallen only a few feet away from her. Blood stained his pale yellow shirt, his face and his hands. In death, his fingers still clutched his weapon. She'd seen dead people before. A few years ago in Reno, she'd witnessed the aftermath of a bloody battle with six victims, but this was the first time she'd seen a man take his last breath and die right in front of her.

Julian came closer and placed his hand on her shoulder. She jerked away. *Don't touch me.* She didn't want to be lulled into false security, not with three murdered men on the floor. Her brain needed to stay sharp.

"You've got spatter on your hand," he said. "Were you injured?"

"This isn't my blood."

"It could very well have been."

He was right! She could have been killed by Damien and his men or by the Baker. The smart thing to do right now was to get away from here as quickly as possible. Maybe she ought to drive straight to the FBI headquarters, admit defeat and end her undercover assignment. For the first time, she considered quitting in the middle of an assignment. On her phone, she had a highly protected app that she could activate with a three-digit code. The signal rang through to the FBI and notified her handler that she was in need of immediate backup. Special agents could track her location using her phone's GPS.

Never before had she thought she'd need those buttons. Calling for help would knock her down a few rungs on the career ladder, and she wouldn't have her choice of assignments. But getting killed on the job wasn't a good alternative.

She wanted to stick with this investigation. Damien had dropped new information that she should check out. He'd mentioned an escaped girl, which indicated that they'd already started the trafficking operations—at least, trial runs—using Nick's. Angie had to stay on the job so she could rescue that girl who might be Cara's playmate. Until Gigi was safe, Angie couldn't quit, but that didn't mean she had to stay right here in the middle of a crime scene. "My car is parked down the block. I'm leaving."

"You're in no condition to drive." Julian pulled a stool over beside the stainless steel table and patted the seat. "Sit. Catch your breath."

"I'm fine. I don't need help." Her standard response. She'd made that claim so many times that she actually believed it was true. She didn't *want* to be dependent, didn't *want* to need him or anybody else.

In an unexpectedly gentle tone, he said, "Let me take care of this."

If only she could believe him! She wanted to take a step back and let her brain rest while somebody else took the initiative and the responsibility. Gazing into his intense blue eyes, she felt safe and reassured.

From her perch on the stool, she watched as Julian checked the other two men to make sure they were all dead. He took out his cellphone and had a conversation. She wondered if he was talking to Lorenzo to get instructions. Or was Julian important enough that he didn't need to consult with the boss?

The Baker lumbered over and stood beside Julian. "This wasn't my fault," he said.

"Okay."

"Damien broke in here. This was a clear case of self-defense. You can ask Angie on account of she saw the whole thing. She's my witness."

"It's all right, my friend. You don't need to worry about witnesses or self-defense," Julian said. "We're not going to tell the police about this."

Ice-cold dread surged through her veins. *No police?* With numb fingers, she checked the safety on her Tomcat to make sure it was ready to fire in case she needed to shoot her way out. As if she could? Running away was a much better idea. If she could slide out of this room and make it to her car, she wouldn't stop driving until she reached the Pacific shores.

Rudy entered the shop from the front. "Hey, Baker, it looks like I missed all the fun."

The young man's bravado wasn't convincing. She noticed a twitch near his eye and guessed that he was nearly as nervous as she was.

"About the other two guys who came with us," Julian said. "Can they be trusted? Before you answer, keep in mind that your uncle will be very disappointed if your buddies start bragging or shooting off their mouths to the cops."

"They're cool," Rudy said.

Julian spoke to the Baker. "Go home and clean up. Take a shower to get the gunshot residue off your skin. Then you should burn your clothes. Your wife will give you an alibi, not that you need one. We will never speak of this night again."

"What am I supposed to do?" Rudy asked.

"You and your crew are in charge of cleanup. There's not much time before Valentino's morning bakers come in to start work. Wipe everything down. Use bleach on the blood. Repair the broken window in the front door."

"Got it," Rudy said. "What's your job?"

"Not that it's any of your damn business, but it's what I always do," Julian said calmly. "I get rid of the bodies."

He stalked across the kitchen toward her. With every step that brought him closer, her heart beat faster. "You don't need to tell me what to do," she said. "I know the drill. I go home, take a shower, burn my clothes and forget this happened."

"You're coming with me."

She most definitely did *not* want to ride along while he dumped the bodies. "But I need to clean up. I've got blood on my jacket."

He took off his glasses and leaned closer. His blue eyes—a liar's eyes—cast a mesmerizing glow, but she had to be immune. She couldn't take a chance on going with him. "You ride with me, Angie."

Turning off her apprehension was impossible, but there was a part of her—the FBI-trained sector of her brain—that told her she needed to hear what he had to say. Julian was a major player in the Lorenzo organization. He might give her information that would unravel all these twists and turns. No matter how scared she was, she had to go with him.

Climbing off the stool, she stood before him and stared up into those incredible eyes. She linked her arm with his. “Lead on.”

WHEN JULIAN ESCORTED Angie to his SUV and held the door open for her, he saw her reluctance in the way she fidgeted. This lady was ready to take off like a jackrabbit, and he couldn’t let that happen before they had a few things straightened out. “Please wait for me in the car,” he said. “And I need to see your purse.”

“Why?”

“Maybe I want to freshen up my lipstick.”

“Not funny and not the right timing. We’re only a few steps away from a murder scene.” She did a *tsk-tsk* like an old lady. “You and Valentino share a very weird sense of humor. Now, tell me why you want my purse.”

“To dispose of your gun,” he said. “I’m guessing that your cellphone and car keys are also in that tiny purse, and I’d feel better with both of those items in my possession.”

“So I can’t run away?”

“Correct.”

“You don’t trust me.”

Before she could make another objection, he lifted her purse from her lap. “Stay here. I’ll be back in a minute.”

He returned to the bakery and gave more detailed orders to Rudy and the other two stooges. They'd found a storage closet at the back of the shop, and it contained the supplies they'd need, including painter's drop cloths to wrap the bodies and a pane of glass to repair the broken window in the front door.

"Use all the cloths," Julian instructed. "I don't want to get too much blood in my car."

"You got it, boss." Rudy stepped up. He was in charge and clearly enjoyed giving orders. "We'll take care of the mess. You tell my uncle I'm doing a good job."

Julian returned to his SUV, got behind the wheel and turned toward her. "Here's your purse, and I brought you something else."

He handed her a small white box printed with the Valentino logo. She immediately opened it. "A cupcake?"

"You're welcome." He started the engine and drove around to the back of the shop where Rudy and his guys could more easily load the bodies. Valentino's van was already gone.

"I don't believe this," she snapped. "Do you really expect me to forgive you because you brought a cupcake?"

"It's chocolate icing."

"In the future, please don't grab my belongings and treat me like a child. If you really needed for me to stay in the car, you could have explained. Like an adult." She flipped open the purse and dug through it. "Where are my car keys?"

"I gave them to Rudy." He maneuvered the SUV so the rear was near the back door of the bakery. "He's going to drive your car to Nick's so we don't have to come back into town to pick it up."

"Totally unacceptable," she said. "I want my keys and my car. And I don't want to ride along with you to dump the bodies." He saw her reach for the door handle and tapped the childproof locking system. She yanked the handle twice before she realized she couldn't get out. "Open this. Open it now."

"For the next hour, I need your undivided attention. I owe you an explanation, and this isn't something I can rattle off in a few quick sentences. It's complicated, and it's important that you understand. Things can get serious when you're working for Lorenzo. Tonight, you saw how bad it can get."

"Three murders. It doesn't get much worse."

"Last night, I promised that I'd protect you. That's what I mean to do."

The side door of the SUV slid open, and Rudy stuck his head inside. "Where do you want them?"

"In the back, and you'll need to collapse the rear seat to make room. I'll pop the lock."

Angie turned so she could see what was going on behind her. In a quiet voice, she said, "What if I don't want your protection?"

"I'm not trying to insult you or say that you're weak. But you're new in town and really don't know what you've gotten yourself into." The car bounced as the first body was loaded into the back. "You might get hurt while you're figuring things out."

"Thanks for your concern but you don't know what's best for me. I've been making my own decisions for a very long time, and I know what I need." She swiveled around in her seat and focused on the windshield. "You might have gotten the wrong impression last night when I was all weepy. I'm not like that."

"I never said you were."

"You think I should stay safe. What does that mean? Wait, let me guess. You think I should keep my head down and do my job at OTB and not make waves. I should be a good girl, an obedient girl. Take no risks. Then I won't get hurt."

In the dim light behind the bakery, he studied her determined expression. When she looked at him, her dark eyes blazed. "I'd never try to tell you not to make waves. That's not your nature. Angie, you're a tsunami."

"You bet I am."

The back of the SUV bounced again as corpse number two was loaded inside. "Give me the chance to explain. Afterward, the decisions are up to you."

"And you'll take me back to my room at Nick's?"

"If that's what you want."

She flipped open the lid on the cupcake box and scooped a bite of frosting. The rumbling sound from the back of her throat sounded like purring. "I love chocolate."

TELLING HER THE whole truth might not be the smartest strategy he'd ever come up with, but his decision was made. He'd meant it when he said she needed to know what kind of mess she'd stumbled into. A clear picture was necessary, but he wasn't anxious to get started with his long, complicated story and wasn't sure how she'd react.

"Question," she said. "When do I get my gun back?"

"Not as long as it can be tied to the murders. Are you attached to the Tomcat?"

"It's a handy size." She licked her lips, savoring every taste of chocolate. "I can't actually remember the last time I fired it."

The third body was dumped inside and the back of the SUV closed with a final click. Rudy tapped on the driver's side window and Julian lowered the glass.

"We're done," Rudy said.

"Good." The kid was proving to be a useful assistant, after all. "When you're finished with the rest of the job, take photos on your phone and send them to me."

"Got it." He stepped out of the way as the SUV pulled forward.

Driving west toward the mountains, Julian should have felt more relieved. The issue of the man with the scar had been permanently settled with Damien's death. Evidence from the crime scene would be erased. And he knew Zapata was not to be trusted.

"I'm ready," Angie said. "Tell me your complicated story."

The truth would shock her. He couldn't just blurt it out. "I'm going to start with what happened three years ago when I joined the construction crew working on the building and renovating at Nick's."

She popped the last bite of cupcake into her mouth

and gave another chocolate purr. "I don't suppose you grabbed another one of these."

"I should have grabbed a dozen." Glancing over at her, he wished she'd invite him to lick the icing from her lips. Thoughts like that made it even more difficult to be honest with her.

"Back to your story," she said. "Once upon a time..."

"This isn't a fairy tale. There's no moral to the story, and I'm pretty sure there isn't a happily-ever-after."

He didn't want to drop this bombshell while they were so close to the bakery and might be followed. Better to wait until...until what? Damn it, there wasn't a good time for him to tell her that he'd been lying from the first moment they'd met. The whole time he'd been accusing her of withholding information and being mysterious, he had his own secrets.

She might betray him, but that was a chance he was willing to take. If she didn't want to cooperate and step away from trouble, he could always have her arrested. That was one of the advantages of his real job as an undercover agent for the Colorado Bureau of Investigation.

Chapter Twelve

The primary purpose of Angie's undercover work was to dig up evidence that would help the FBI shut down illegal operations and lock criminals away. Though she hadn't been following a detailed plan with Lorenzo, she must have been doing something right because here she was, riding along with Julian, who wanted to tell her his deepest, darkest secrets. As a high-ranking member of Lorenzo's organization, he had access to information that could seriously damage the start-up of a trafficking operation.

She should have been hanging on his every word but didn't really want to hear what he had to say. What if he felt compelled to confess to her? *Oh, the irony!* She liked this guy and didn't want to arrest him.

He was driving the same route that he took on the day they met. She remembered how nervous she'd been, imagining all the terrible things that could happen to her in the mountains. Now she was calm. *Another irony!* The bodies of three murdered men were tucked into the space behind her.

"Where are we going?" she asked.

"I have a place I generally use for things like this."

The thought that he had a special body dumping site should have terrified her. Why wasn't she frantically plotting her escape from him? "That's another joke, right?"

"Here's what I want you to know," he said. "I was a carpenter before I met Lorenzo on the job site for Nick's. We discussed architecture and found out that we had similar tastes, which resulted in incorporating some of my ideas in the project. I took over the supervising of several crews. Long story short, I ended up working for him on a more permanent basis."

She understood what he was trying to tell her in his roundabout way. "You didn't intend to start out as a criminal."

"Exactly."

Not much of a defense. If he was such an innocent participant in Lorenzo's business, how did he become the go-to guy for dumping bodies? *We all make our own decisions.* That was a painful lesson she'd discovered many years ago: take responsibility for your actions.

But she didn't climb up on her pulpit to lecture him. What good would it do to make accusations or insinuate that he was a bad guy? Though she hadn't seen a dangerous side to Julian, she knew better than to poke a sleeping grizzly.

He continued, "I'm not part of the inner circle, never was. Sure, I have a lot of responsibility. Nick's is an important part of the overall business, but Lorenzo doesn't tell me everything. He and Zapata and the rest of them stood back and watched me spin while I was searching for Damien."

The SUV exited the highway on the right and followed a narrow road that she thought would take them through Morrison and then into the wide valley where Red Rocks Amphitheatre was located. She didn't like this deviation from standard procedure, and worried about the way he was constantly checking the rearview mirrors as though expecting to see the headlights of another car following them.

She glanced over her shoulder toward the rear window, trying not to look at the bodies wrapped in drop cloths. "I haven't been this way before."

"Scenic route," he said as though that explained everything. "We're actually headed back to Denver."

"What about…" She nodded toward their terrible cargo. "Don't you have to do something about them?"

"I've got it covered."

For some unexplainable reason, his vague promise didn't trigger a panic attack. Her pulse was steady and strong, which made her think that he'd hypnotized her with his electric-blue eyes and tousled hair. The facts pointed to danger, especially with the way he kept looking for a tail, but she felt safe.

Telling herself not to be an idiot, she eased her phone out of her purse. This might be the right time to punch in that code and call for FBI backup. Holding her phone at the ready, she leaned back in the passenger seat and watched the scenery unfold. Even at night, Red Rocks was impressive. Not that she was in the mood for sightseeing.

"Here's the thing, Julian. You're trying to soften the blow by easing into your explanation, like pulling the bandage off slowly. But I'm not a patient woman. I'm more of a rip-it-off-fast person. Just tell me what I need to know."

"When I took that carpentry job, I thought it was just a couple weeks' work but I'm glad it turned out the way it did. Managing Nick's is the best job I've ever had. I'm going to miss it."

"Are you planning to quit?"

"I have to." He seemed to relax behind the wheel, satisfied that they were the only ones on the road. "There's no choice."

"Is that what you want to tell me? That you're quitting?"

"That's part of it, but—"

"Tell me," she demanded. "If you don't explain real soon, I'm going to scream like a tone-deaf opera diva."

"A threat?"

"You don't want to hear my high C."

"From the moment we met," he said. "I've been lying to you. And it's not just you. I've lied to everybody."

If she hadn't been the self-proclaimed Queen of Deception, she might have been more shocked. "I'm going to need a little bit more."

"I'm not really an architect or a carpenter or a criminal. I work for the Colorado Bureau of Investigation, the CBI, and I've been undercover at Nick's. I feed information to law enforcement so they can swoop in and make arrests."

She didn't know whether to laugh or cry. He was never going to believe that she was his mirror reflection, working for the FBI. "Why tell me? Aren't you worried that I'll rat you out to Lorenzo?"

"You could." He guided the SUV onto the highway leading back to Denver. "It's a risk I'm willing to take. There's something big going down at Nick's, and I don't want you to get caught in the crossfire."

Hadn't she told him a dozen times that she could protect herself? His big confession was a little bit insulting to her. "What else?"

"The CBI can get Marigold into protective custody."

The Colorado Bureau was nothing compared to the feds. Julian might think he had all the answers, but this wasn't his call. Who did he think he was? Her irritation spiked. She had a stake in this game, and she had the juice to make sure everything turned out right—more power than he had. Maybe she hadn't been undercover with Lorenzo for three years, but she had experience. Angie punched the three-digit code into her phone and followed up with a text. It was time for Julian to meet her FBI handler.

INSTEAD OF DRIVING to a secluded mountain dump site and digging shallow graves for the three murdered men, they went to the downtown Denver morgue used by the CBI for autopsies. Angie was somewhat impressed that Julian was able to make these arrangements with a few phone calls. He parked his SUV on a subterranean level under a huge hospital complex where a gang of medical people in scrubs and lab coats were waiting with gurneys to transport the corpses—a messy process but it would have been worse if rigor had set in. When they moved Damien to the gurney, the cloth fell back from his face. His mouth gaped, revealing yellowed teeth. His skin was waxen, and the discolored scar across his forehead stood out in sharp relief.

Though Angie would shed no tears for this man who had assaulted Waylon and terrorized Jane, she silently offered a prayer that he would be at peace. No one deserved to die from violence. She looked toward Julian. "What happens next?"

"The bodies are signed in with the coroner. Autopsies will be required."

Since the cause of death was not a question, she guessed that these three would not be high priority. Still, an autopsy could yield a wealth of information, ranging from tattoos to medical conditions related to where the deceased lived. "When will they have the preliminary DNA results?"

"Soon," he said. "They need to get an ID and check the criminal data base."

"I know." She was familiar with standard procedure. "I was asking about specific timing. The autopsy doctors probably don't work at night. Does somebody else take DNA samples and run facial recognition?"

He eyed her suspiciously. "How do you know about what happens in the morgue?"

"I watch crime shows on TV." Not revealing her identity was akin to lying, and she was comfortable in this zone. Angie couldn't wait to see the look on his face when he found out she was a fed.

A tall, lean man with a full head of gray hair and tired eyes approached them. Julian introduced him as

Supervisory Special Agent Shanahan, the ranking officer in the CBI. When Angie shook his hand, she was acutely aware of the blood spatter on her sleeve. Gunshot residue wasn't visible to the naked eye, but her clothes and hands must be covered with it. She didn't kill the unnamed third man, but she'd shot him.

SSA Shanahan directed them into the building past a couple of labs and into a nondescript office. He sat behind the desk and took out a recording device. After stating his name and her alias, he made eye contact with Julian and asked, "How much does Ms. D'Angelo know about your situation?"

"She knows I'm an agent," he said. "It's okay to use my name."

"Special Agent Julian Parish aka Parisi," Shanahan said. "Tell me what happened tonight."

While he described his surveillance at Nick's and how he'd picked up visual recognition of Damien in the casino, she rolled both of his names around in her head. Changing the final *i* to an *h* transformed her expectations in surprising ways. Parisi was more musical and exotic, but Parish suited him better. Julian Parish seemed like the kind of guy who sat in the front of the class and wore glasses. If that image was true and he actually was a kind of nerd, Julian was a better liar than she gave him credit for. In spite of her attraction to him, she'd believed he was a dangerous badass.

He wrapped up his narrative at the point in time when he drove into the front parking area for Valentino's bakery. Both Julian and SSA Shanahan focused on her. It only took a few moments for her to tell what had happened inside the bakery. There was really no good way to express the intensity she'd felt in those moments when she faced death and made the decision to shoot. Three men had died.

When she looked down at her hands in her lap, she noticed a slight tremor. *This won't do!* Covering her tension, she adjusted her ponytail and smoothed her hair. "That's all."

"I might have missed something," SSA Shanahan said. "Did you tell us why you went to the bakery at midnight?"

"I needed to order a cake." She glanced from Shanahan to Julian, reading disbelief on their faces. "Valentino believed me so there's no reason for you guys to be skeptical. I needed a cake for a special event."

"Had you made an appointment with him?" Shanahan asked.

"Of course not, midnight is a ridiculous time for an appointment."

"What's your relationship with Valentino? Are you close?"

Did he seriously consider her a suspect? She couldn't resist playing with SSA Shanahan. Leaning across the desk, she licked her lips, still tasting the chocolate icing. "Let's just say that I love Valentino's baked goods."

"How long have you known him?"

"I met him at the same time I met Julian."

"Okay," Shanahan said. "You had no long-term connection."

For the third time that night, she took out her phone and checked the app that connected with the FBI. She'd been texting back and forth with her handler. His last message told her that he'd arrived and was outside this office, waiting for her instructions.

She spun around and crossed the room. With her hand on the doorknob, she said, "There's someone here who can explain."

Though she'd never met Special Agent Hemming in person, she recognized him from his online profile. In the FBI, undercover operatives didn't show up online, didn't post photos and didn't take selfies. Their real names and backgrounds were guarded. As she approached SA Hemming, she held up her phone to show him the app and assure him that she was who she claimed to be. "Call me Angie."

He shook her hand and touched the brim of his cowboy hat. "You're not what I expected."

"I'm better, right?"

"You're something."

A big guy with an easy smile, Hemming was dressed in what she assumed was the Wild West version of "men in black"—black jeans, white shirt with bolo tie and a black jacket with fringe. He got directly to the point. "How can I help?"

She ushered him into the office where she introduced Julian and SSA Shanahan. "This is Special Agent Hemming of the FBI. This unlucky man is assigned to be my handler."

"Your handler?" Julian blurted.

"Our two agencies need better communication to avoid this sort of redundancy," she said, keeping her tone calm and even. "Like you, I'm undercover."

SSA Shanahan reacted with smooth professionalism as he shook hands with Hemming. "We're always happy to work with the FBI."

Julian was nowhere near as cool. Behind his glasses, his eyes bulged like a pair of solid blue, number two pool balls. His jaw tensed, and she could tell that he was gritting his teeth. This human volcano was about to spew. She almost felt sorry for him…almost.

Chapter Thirteen

There were times in Julian's life when he wished the floor would open and swallow him whole. *I'm an ass, a total ass.* He sat in the square institutional chair in the small office down the hall from the morgue and tensed every muscle to keep from cringing. These dull beige walls were closing in and crushing him. In his mind, he replayed every dopey comment he'd made about how she couldn't protect herself. His questions about her background and whether she was dating Manny Harris, a DEA agent, must have sounded as naive as a third grader. Less than an hour ago, he'd made his great big declaration that he was CBI undercover. *What a joke!*

Angie sashayed across the office, stopped behind his chair and leaned close to his ear. "You must have had some idea that I was a cop..."

Didn't have a clue. When he'd learned about her connection to Marigold, he'd thought Angie's secret, unstated motivation for all her lies was revenge against Lorenzo.

She continued. "Right away, you knew that I wasn't who I claimed to be. That was smart deduction on your part because my online profile and data were constructed by the geniuses in FBI cybercrimes."

Was that the truth or was she patronizing him? "You're a good liar."

"So are you."

And he was done feeling sorry for himself.

Abruptly, he stood. With an emphatic sweep of his hand, he shoved away all doubt and confusion. Whether or not she played him for a fool didn't matter. He'd been working this undercover identity for three years, and he'd be damned if he allowed Nick's to be turned into a hub for trafficking. He whipped off his glasses and stared down at her. When he spoke, his voice dropped to a low, authoritative level.

"Since we'll be working together," he said, "we need a plan to avoid bumping heads."

"What do you suggest?" she asked.

"I'll continue meeting with Lorenzo, Valentino and the Zapatas—both Nolan and Carlos. Maybe I can get them to open up about Damien and his role in the trafficking operation."

"I've got ideas of my own," she said. "Tomorrow, I want to take Cara into the hills behind the bunkhouse and search for the friend she calls Gigi. If this child exists and escaped from a prior trafficking attempt, she'll have useful info. I'm also going to meet with Marigold."

"I'll come with you to search," he said.

"Not a good idea. This little girl might be scared of men."

"Sure." He sucked down an angry breath. "But won't

she be frightened when confronted by a woman on horseback who doesn't know how to ride?"

Before she could snap back at him, he noticed that her handler and his supervisor had put their heads together. They were grinning, nodding and shaking hands. He doubted their alliance would bode well for him or Angie.

Hemming came toward them. In spite of his mountainous size, he moved athletically. When he sat on the edge of the desk, Julian hoped the old wooden furniture would support Hemming's weight. "You two have made errors," Hemming said, "starting with those three dead men in the coroner's office. It would have been better to take them alive so we could interrogate and get information."

"You're right," Angie said.

He appreciated the fact that she didn't try to hide behind excuses. Julian added, "While I was studying the surveillance on Damien, I noticed a skull tat on the back of his hand and three *H*s on his fingers."

"Good catch," Hemming said. "The *H* tattoos stand for a cartel that started in Colombia and now operates from Juarez. I expect we'll find similar markings on the other two men."

"It's a start," Julian said.

"You're good at your job, Parish. Shanahan tells me that your intelligence is responsible for major disruptions in black market drug sales, illegal gun smuggling and a prostitution ring." He turned his head to focus on Angie. "This woman has equally impressive accomplishments, including the recovery of eight million dollars in jewelry and art."

"But don't either of you get bigheaded," Shanahan said. "But we don't want to shut down either of your investigations. You're going to work together. And you'll stay in touch with us through dedicated, encoded apps. Got it?"

He and Angie responded with a simultaneous, "Yes sir."

They were on the same page, which was good. And the investigation seemed straightforward. This situation might not be too miserable.

SSA Shanahan said, "We've come up with an undercover story that will allow you to spend more time together and not look suspicious."

Hemming beamed. "We want you two to pretend to be lovers."

Julian's momentary sense of well-being was gone. He and Angie would be undercover lovers? This plan had disaster written all over it.

TWO HOURS LATER, they were back in the SUV headed for Nick's. Jostling along in the passenger seat, Angie didn't dare close her eyes for even a second for fear that she'd drift into a deep sleep. The coffee they'd picked up from a hospital vending machine tasted like sludge, but the caffeine jolt was welcome.

She was just alert enough to notice that Nick had taken I-70, which was the long way around. "Why this route?" she asked.

"I want to approach from the west so it looks like I went deeper into the mountains to bury the bodies."

She groaned. "Do you really think anybody will notice?"

"I like to be prepared for any and all possibilities. Whether or not anybody is watching, I'm covered. I also didn't wash the blood out of the back. Cleaning my SUV is a job for one of the valets."

"Earlier tonight when you took that weird detour past Red Rocks, did you think somebody might be following you?"

"I always drive as if somebody's on my tail, using extreme caution. That's why I've lasted three years at this assignment. I don't take chances." He glanced in her direction. "I'm not like you."

"What's that supposed to mean?"

"Come on, Angie, you know what I'm talking about. You're lucky Valentino didn't blow your head off when you showed up on his doorstep and started talking about cake."

"He bought it," she pointed out.

"He bought the whole package, believing that you're a pretty blonde who is kind of ditzy. The act works for you, and that's not a bad thing. But there aren't many people who can pull off that kind of con job."

She preferred to think of her approach as intuitive. Based on her intelligence and training, she charged in the right direction. If she stumbled into trouble, she used her skill at lying to escape. Still, she appreciated his ability to think ahead. "Planning is good. I promise not to jump into anything without talking to you first."

"What was the real reason you went to the bakery?"

"I wanted to look for evidence in his delivery truck. Based on a bit of conversation I overheard, I think those vehicles are being used for trafficking."

"Makes sense."

An uncomfortable moment of silence stretched between them. They'd been lying to each other for days and had no basis for trust. Also, when you got right down to the bottom line, they were rivals. He worked for the state, and she was a fed.

She imagined he was protective of his turf, and she understood why he'd feel that way. The same didn't apply to her. Though she liked to finish what she started, Angie wasn't deeply invested in Nick's. "You know, if I wasn't so concerned about Marigold, I'd be happy to step aside and let you handle everything."

"You don't seriously expect me to believe your story about Marigold, do you?"

Did he think she was faking her breakdown when he found her on the balcony outside Marigold's bedroom? "It's the truth."

"I'm going to assume that every word you've said to me is a lie, including that. Now, about this undercover lover thing...we need to figure out how to handle it."

"No big deal. We'll hold hands and give each other longing looks."

"Not enough," he said. "Nick's is like a small town with everybody watching everybody else all the time. The place runs on gossip. It's going to take more than a peck on the cheek to convince them that we've got something going."

"You think?"

"Tonight, when I park at the curb outside Nick's and come around to open your door, you need to kiss me. I want a real kiss, a big one."

"With tongue?"

"You bet, and we should go to the same room as though we're sleeping together. I suggest we use my suite because it's bigger."

This had to be the most clinical proposition she'd ever received. "Sorry, Julian, but that's a negative. It's my room, nonnegotiable."

"Why?"

"I don't want to get up in the morning and do the 'walk of shame' down to the concierge level. It's a lousy way to start the day."

"But it's okay for me to do the walk?"

"Men don't feel shame," she said. "They strut."

He laughed, and she was relieved to hear his chuckle—a sign that they were beginning to adjust to the crazy new reality that had been foisted upon them by his SSA and her handler. "I want you to know," she said, "that this lover thing is new for me. I've never seduced a man as part of an undercover operation. My platinum blond hair, the jewelry and bedazzled clothes aren't meant to attract male attention. I think of my outfits as armor."

"Yeah, you're real scary."

In the distancc, she could see the lights from the parking lot and from outside the seven-story wings. The neon Nick's logo gleamed red. At this hour on a Sunday night, the lobby and entrance were still lit, but most of the hotel windows were dark. "Is the casino open all night?"

"The casino and some of the restaurants. They're open but not very busy," He drove into the driveway. "Remember, Angie, we're going to give the valets a show. Don't hold back."

Kissing him wasn't the worst thing that she'd done on an assignment. They had chemistry, and Julian was a good-looking man. Not that handsome was any guarantee of sexual talent. A great kiss needed pressure, a friction, penetration by the tongue and taste—all wrapped up in a Goldilocks package with not too much and not too little.

She dug into her purse, grabbed a tin of mints and popped one into her mouth. She offered one to him and was glad when he took two. Was he as nervous about this as she was?

At the entrance, Julian parked and climbed out from behind the wheel. As he circled the car, she watched him give instructions to the two valets on duty, no doubt telling them to scrub the interior of his car and use bleach to erase the bloodstains. Julian's posture was strong and upright. He moved with the confidence of an alpha male.

When he approached the passenger side, he removed his glasses and tucked them into the inner pocket of his jacket. The door opened, and he took her hand to help her out. Though she was perfectly capable of bounding from the car and racing him to the entrance, she enjoyed the civilized gesture. She stood on the sidewalk, gazing into his amazing blue eyes encircled by dark lashes. He might have been grinning, but she didn't know for sure. The eyes captured her absolute attention.

"Very gentlemanly," she said.

"You're my lady."

Somewhat corny, but his words twanged an unthinking, visceral response inside her. A wave of excitement rippled from her scalp to her toes as his arm wrapped around her waist. He tightened his grasp until her body pressed flush against his chest. Her head tilted back, and her lips parted.

His mouth brushed hers, tentative at first and then he connected and increased the pressure so she had to respond. When his tongue swept against her teeth, she opened wider and welcomed him inside. He tasted of mint.

The main action stayed at the mouth, but she was aware of rubbing against him. Her hands slid inside his jacket and climbed his strong, muscular back. Though he was at least six inches taller than her five foot nine, they fit together nicely.

When he ended the kiss, her knees were weak. *Best assignment I've ever had.* She needed to send bouquets of roses to Hemming and Shanahan.

Julian kept his arm around her as they crossed the lobby and went to the elevators. The door whooshed open, and he escorted her inside. Before the elevator door could close, he held her face in both of his hands and leaned close. Under his breath, he said, "Surveillance camera. Kiss me again."

She didn't need another invitation. This should have been a quick kiss, only a few seconds, but when the doors opened on the fourth floor, Julian wouldn't let them close. Using his foot, he blocked the elevator and continued to kiss her while the bong-bong-bong warning bell clanged.

When they stepped onto the floor, a husky concierge leaned against the front of his desk with his thumbs hitched into the pockets of his jeans. He watched them with a bemused grin. Taking a moment, she straightened her clothes. Quietly, she mumbled, "I forgot about all the cameras."

"That's why I'm here," he said. "Planning."

"Well, Mr. Planner, you're lucky I remembered not to put on a fresh coat of lipstick. With all this kissing, you'd look like a clown right now."

Julian stopped to talk to the guy at the desk while she gave him a wave and continued on to her suite. The living room was decorated in a southwestern motif with a sitting area, a desk by the window and a kitchenette. The bedroom was furnished with two queen-size beds, which meant she wouldn't be forced to sleep with him. *Too bad.* She wouldn't have minded taking this charade all the way…or would she?

In the bathroom, she took down her ponytail and massaged her scalp. Tonight had been intense—from the murders to the revelation about Julian, to the new undercover assignment, to the kiss. She needed to take a step back and figure out what was going on.

Julian tapped on the bathroom door. "I'm going to sweep the suite to make sure there aren't any new cameras or mics."

"Knock yourself out."

"Are you okay?"

"Never better."

For the tiniest sliver of a second, she considered inviting him into the bathroom to share her shower, but that was a step she didn't dare take. In her line of work, she couldn't maintain a long-term committed relationship. And Julian didn't fit the profile for a fling or a one-night stand.

Chapter Fourteen

Last night, Julian had hoped for more—more physical contact, more talking and more getting to know his undercover lover. But when he entered the bedroom, he found Angie sprawled across the sheets, sound asleep. Those two hot, steamy kisses should have led to more, and it seemed like she'd been making an effort to be sexy in an ice-blue satin nightie that hugged her curves and showed off her cleavage.

He'd stretched out on the bed beside her and watched her sleep. Without makeup, her face was fresh and sweet. She hadn't tamed her hair into a ponytail or a bun, and her unbridled platinum mane spilled across the pillow. He'd kissed her lightly on the forehead but decided not to wake her. They both needed sleep.

With morning light seeping into the room, he stood over her bed, once again gazing down at her peaceful form. Though he told himself that there would be time for him to kiss her soft lips and gradually get to know her body as a lover should, he had no guarantee. Time was not under his control. The trafficking operation could spring into action at any moment, and their assignment would be over. He needed to take advantage of every minute alone with her. And yet, he stepped back.

At eight o'clock on a Monday morning, he needed to get started on the week's business at Nick's and to shove his investigation forward. The murders last night had flipped everything into high gear. With great reluctance, he exited her suite, being careful to close the door quietly. When he turned, he saw Muscleman Matt McHenry standing in front of the concierge desk. Was he smirking? Beside him, Cara watched Julian through suspicious eyes. This must be what Angie meant when she referred to the "walk of shame," not that Julian had anything to be ashamed of. He straightened his shoulders and walked toward the concierge and his perky companion.

"Did you have a sleepover with Angie?" Cara asked.

That was an accurate description of last night's activity or the lack thereof. "We were both tired. And we slept."

Cara dismissed him with a shrug and jumped to another topic. "Angie's going for a riding lesson today, and I'm going with her."

Last night, Julian had told the concierge on duty that the guy who had been menacing Cara and her mom was dead. Still, he wanted them to stay here and have full protection. He glanced at McHenry whose sheer body mass was enough to deter most assailants. "I want you to go with them."

"I can manage that." When he looked down at Cara, his rugged features softened. Somehow, the kid had melted his firm resolve. "Yesterday, Cara and Jane and

I went into the hills for target practice. I'm thinking of getting a bullwhip of my own."

A strange way to bond, but Julian had no room to judge. He said, "I'll try to join you for the lesson."

"Yes!" Cara shouted, and then she dashed toward him and jumped into his arms for a hug. "We can have an adventure."

He hoped there wouldn't be too much excitement.

AFTER JULIAN WENT to his suite, showered and shaved, and ordered breakfast from room service, he was ready to face the day. His first stop was his office where he could deal with the myriad issues that usually popped up over the weekend. No sooner had he settled behind his desk than Tamara Rigby entered with a mug of fragrant black coffee and a folder that she dropped into his inbox tray. Though she wore her official hotel uniform of blazer, slacks and crisp white shirt, she had retained some of the glamour from her night at the Glass Palace. Her lipstick was bright, and her mossy green eyes sparkled.

"I had a wonderful time on Saturday," she said. "It's too bad that you and Angie had to leave early."

"I hope Leif took good care of you."

"He was so sweet." She exhaled a heavy sigh. "Most people see him as a big, tough football star, but he's intelligent and sensitive. We like a lot of the same music and same movies. Can you believe it? I have something in common with Leif."

He sipped his coffee, which was—as almost everything Tamara did—perfectly flavored and exactly the right temperature. This woman really was a catch. He nodded, encouraging her to continue talking. Her gossip was a welcome distraction from the horrifying scene he'd encountered at Valentino's. In contrast, things had been quiet at Nick's.

Soon, he'd have to leave this job. In the course of investigation, his role as an undercover operative would be exposed. Of course, he wouldn't be able to work for Lorenzo, and it was likely that Nick's would be altogether closed down. Julian wished for a different conclusion.

When he started as a carpenter at Nick's, the plan had been for him to spend a few weeks at the job to see if he could discover inside information. In less than a week, he'd heard delivery times for a massive drug deal and enough dirt to bury a local politician. SSA Shanahan decided that he should stay on the job for another couple of weeks. Then Lorenzo offered him a permanent position and the rest, as they say, was history.

Three years was a long stretch for an undercover assignment but not a waste of time. Julian had cemented his status as one of Lorenzo's top advisors, and he had contact with most of the other criminals in the state of Colorado and beyond. When this was over, he could provide enough intel to wipe the slate clean. The downside: he couldn't possibly continue in undercover work. Too many people knew him as the Professor, Julian Parisi. Going back to his job at the CBI meant riding a desk or sitting in front of a computer screen.

He wrapped his conversation with Tamara with a

final word of caution. "Don't let your common sense get swept away by a handsome football player."

"I won't make that mistake." But her glittering smile told him that she couldn't wait to sink her teeth into the former Bronco. "We have a date for Thursday night after the NFL game."

"Isn't that kind of late?"

"That's the point." She winked.

Julian didn't completely trust Leif. Though he couldn't pinpoint a specific display of disloyalty, his cop instincts warned him that Leif was trouble. If those were the same instincts that wrongly told him Angie couldn't be trusted, and was a criminal, he might be wise to ignore them. She'd turned out to be a fed. Leif might be some other breed of hero.

No more time for second-guessing, Julian needed to focus hard on the trafficking, to take a deep dive. It was time for him to swim with the sharks. After a last sip of coffee, he stood behind his desk and asked Tamara, "Is there anything in that folder that requires immediate attention?"

She shrugged. "Just the usual."

He checked his watch. At a few minutes past nine, it wasn't too early to make the drive into Denver and confront Zapata in his office. "I'll be gone for most of the morning," he said. "You're in charge."

"What if Rudy shows up?"

"I gave him the morning off. He worked late last night." After the cleanup at Valentino's, Rudy had sent photos on his phone. He and his team had done a good job, wiping away the bloody evidence of three murders.

"If he shows, give him some invoices to sign. Enough busywork to make him feel important."

Before leaving his office, he called ahead to the valet station so they could bring his car around to the front. Julian was definitely going to miss the perks and privileges of being boss. Before he got behind the steering wheel, he checked the back of his SUV, which had been perfectly cleaned and detailed. He peeled off a hundred dollar tip to go with the hundred from last night.

While making the familiar drive into Denver, he considered the issues he needed to talk about. The fact that Zapata had kept Damien's identity a secret hinted at a lack of trust. Julian wasn't being informed about the trafficking operation, and he needed to find out why. What was his place in the Lorenzo hierarchy? They couldn't just dump him…or could they? Julian was confident that nobody else could run Nick's as effectively as he could, but he wasn't sure Zapata felt the same way.

His thoughts skipped to the attack on Valentino and then to his surveillance of Damien. What was Lorenzo's position on Zapata and trafficking? Julian's stream of logical thinking came to a screeching halt when he conjured up a sweet vision of Angie in her satin nightie with her hair cascading across the pillow in a platinum wave. He lingered on that fantasy, imagining her lashes fluttering open and her dark eyes gazing up at him. He should have joined her in bed last night, should have stayed in her bedroom this morning. Facing off with Zapata was a lousy alternative.

At ten minutes after ten, he stopped at the secretary's

desk on the top floor of the office building where he'd first met Angie. "Is Zapata in?"

"You should have made an appointment, Julian."

He pushed his glasses up on his nose and gave the secretary a warm smile, hoping to melt her standard show of hostility. She proudly guarded access to Zapata. Nobody got buzzed into the inner office without her approval. "You're right," he said. "I apologize for not following procedure."

"There are reasons for these rules." Though the cut of her pin-striped suit was fashionable, her tone reminded him of a disapproving librarian chastising a student about a late return. "His schedule is booked all day long, and he simply doesn't have a free minute."

Ever since he'd quoted *Pride and Prejudice* to her, he had been one of her favorites. To tell the truth, he felt the same way about her. "Give me a break, Lucille."

"It wouldn't be fair," she said.

"But I drove all the way down from the mountains."

She tapped her pen on the desktop and rearranged her calendar so the edges were precisely parallel to the edge of the desk. When she looked up at him, her pinched lips loosened into a sly grin. "I suppose I could make an exception for you. Just this once."

He suspected that she'd always intended to open the door. He respected the game she played. "Thank you, Lucille."

"I hear you have a girlfriend."

How had the gossip gotten here so fast? "I do," he said. "In some ways, she reminds me of you."

"How so?"

"She's smart and tough and doesn't put up with rudeness. She nearly broke Murph's arm for being impolite."

"I like her already," Lucille said.

He went to the closed double doors and waited for the buzz before he pushed them open. The huge corner office was surrounded by a wide terrace with two floor-to-ceiling windows. One faced south and framed a distant view of Pikes Peak. The other looked east toward the skyline of downtown Denver.

Zapata sat at a glass-topped table on the terrace, drinking coffee that Julian knew would be too strong for his taste. Also seated at the table were Carlos and Rudy. Sharing morning coffee and a plate of doughnuts with Carlos seemed natural. The two of them were family. But the presence of Rudy made him think of one word: *traitor.* Dressed in the same suit he'd worn at the Glass Palace party, Rudy Lorenzo sat straight and self-important, staring into the blue Colorado skies toward the shiny outline of the city.

Julian was angry and tried hard not to show it. He strode across the terrace and stood at the railing. Last night, he'd thought Rudy might be a decent assistant, after all. The kid and his crew had cleaned up the mess without complaint. Before that, during the evening, he'd planted himself in the surveillance room with Julian and watched Damien as he meandered through the casino. Had Rudy known that Damien worked for Zapata?

Though Julian was primed to ask questions and demand answers from his treacherous assistant, he focused instead on Zapata and Carlos. They were important and responsible for decisions while Rudy was nothing more than a punk.

He walked to a chair at the table but didn't sit. His direct focus rested on Zapata, and he tempered his rage with a social comment. "Did you enjoy your birthday party?"

"I don't feel like I'm sixty."

His thick hair hadn't gotten the news. Not a single strand of gray disrupted the shiny black helmet. "You look well."

"The secret is getting enough sleep."

"I didn't rest well last night. Your boy, Damien, caused a disruption."

"You'll get over it."

Zapata sipped from his mug and patted his mouth with a cloth napkin. Today, he wore a casual jacket over a shirt with an open collar and jeans. In spite of occasional flashes from the precious stones in his heavy gold rings, he looked like the ace accountant that he was. Everything with Zapata was based on P&L statement with emphasis on the *profit*.

"You should have told me," Julian said. "When I first reported that somebody attacked Waylon in the barn, you should have told me that Damien worked for you. Searching for him was a time suck. Those are hours I'll never get back."

Carlos waded into the conversation. "Our association with Damien didn't work out the way we'd hoped."

"Well, it wasn't good for him, either." Damien was murdered, dead, gone.

"Let it go," Carlos advised.

He didn't expect Zapata to apologize. That wasn't the way this guy operated. But Julian needed to get him to open up and deliver some useful information, specifically the details about the trafficking. "You owe me an explanation."

Zapata jolted to his feet. "I owe you nothing."

"You've got something going on," he said. "And I understand Nick's better than anybody. Let me help."

"You make a point." Carlos looked toward his uncle. "You both have something to say, but I think we're all on the same page. Last night, we ran into a problem, a misunderstanding."

"Three murders," Julian said.

"Could have been worse. The Baker wasn't hurt." Carlos gestured for both of them to sit. "It's all taken care of now. Settle down."

Before he sat, Julian pulled back his chair, leaving room for him to bolt if necessary. "When Damien and his gang showed up at Valentino's, was he acting on your orders?"

Carlos held up his palm to block that line of questions. "We would never order a hit on Valentino. Damien worked for a group we're doing business with, and the arrogant little weasel got it into his head that he could handle logistics better than us. Basically, this was a disagreement about transportation issues."

Julian put two and two together. Angie's suspicion that Valentino's delivery vans would be used to move human cargo made sense. Damien must have figured that if he eliminated Valentino, he could take over that part of the business. "That still doesn't explain why he attacked Waylon."

"Another can of worms," Carlos said. "Damien was a troublemaker. Now he's gone."

Zapata nodded. "It's good that Damien is out of the picture."

Now they'd gotten to the meat. "Tell me about this picture, the big picture. What project was Damien working on?"

"Back off, man. Don't you ever give up?" Rudy gave a snort that he probably thought was clever. "Zapata already told you that this is none of your business."

"I'm not talking to you, Rudy."

"That's a dumbass mistake. You need to pay attention to me."

"You want attention? Fine. Yesterday, when you and I were in surveillance together, watching Damien, did you know who he was?"

"Maybe."

"Yes or no."

"All right, yes."

"You didn't tell me. You sat and watched while I was spinning my wheels and going nowhere fast."

"So what if I did?"

"You're fired," Julian said.

Rudy jumped from his chair. For a moment, it looked like the kid intended to vault across the table in some kind of airborne assault. Julian was ready for him. He stood, balanced his weight on the balls of his feet and braced for a fight. Usually he avoided physical contact, but Rudy deserved a knock on his pinhead. Not only had he been stupid but he was also disrespectful.

Before Rudy could charge, they heard Lorenzo's voice. "That's enough."

Julian didn't know if he'd been standing there the whole time and watching or if he'd just arrived on the terrace. Either way, his timing was outstanding. He'd avoided the pettiness of the argument but knew exactly where everybody stood. When he strode out of the shadow toward the table, sunlight glittered off the silver mane that contrasted his perfect tan.

The next step, Julian decided, would be his. Since his position at Nick's was already precarious, he might as well risk all the chips.

"I'm glad to see you," Julian said. "I need answers about the project Damien was working on. If I know what's going on, I'll help. On the other hand, if you don't feel like you can tell me, I'll consider it a vote of no confidence."

"What are you saying?" Lorenzo asked.

Julian made the big bet. He went all in. "Tell me or I quit."

"Nobody ever meant to insult you." Lorenzo crossed the terrace toward him. "You haven't been part of our family as long as Zapata or Carlos. And you're not connected by blood like my idiot nephew. But I appreciate the work you've done."

"Best job I've ever had." Julian wasn't playing games and he wasn't lying.

Lorenzo stood only a few feet away. "When the time

is right, I'll tell you exactly what's going on. Until then, I have to ask you to trust me."

"I can't have random thugs like Damien roughing up my employees."

"Understood, and I only need one change in your regular routine. Starting on Tuesday, the night shift in the barn and outbuildings will be handled by three men who don't work for you."

"Tuesday? As in tomorrow?"

"Do you have a problem with that?"

Julian swallowed hard. Tomorrow was too soon. He couldn't possibly get control of the situation by tomorrow night. It took every shred of his self-control to stay cool. "No problem."

"I'll have these men introduce themselves before they start. During the day, the procedure is as usual. Nothing changes. You're still the manager. Waylon takes care of day operations in the barn."

"And at night?"

"My other crew is in charge, and your employees shouldn't be anywhere in sight."

He held out his hand, and Julian had no choice but to take it. Fighting to suppress his panic, he met Lorenzo's gaze and changed the subject. "I fired your idiot nephew."

"I heard."

"If he apologizes, I'll take him back."

Lorenzo gave a nod and stepped aside. Instructions to Rudy were unnecessary. The kid knew what he was supposed to do, and he shuffled forward and told Julian that he was sorry and would never disrespect him again.

The situation with Rudy was nothing compared to the information Lorenzo had revealed. His men would be stationed in the barn at night. The change was scheduled for Tuesday, which meant he and Angie needed to be ready to deal with the traffickers by tomorrow night.

Chapter Fifteen

Angie had always preferred to work alone. Inviting other people into her sometimes elaborate undercover deceptions often resulted in confusion and hampered her ability to think on her feet. As soon as she woke and realized that Julian wasn't in bed with her, she concentrated on what needed to happen today. Her riding lesson in the early afternoon was actually a chance to search for Gigi. The murder of three potential witnesses made it even more important to find the girl who might provide living testimony against the traffickers.

After the Gigi search, Angie would meet with Marigold. Anticipation flooded through her. She'd waited eleven years for this moment, and she feared the outcome might not be what she wanted. Marigold might be the witness who could take down Lorenzo or she might refuse to turn on the man who gave her fancy houses and jewelry. This was definitely a big day, and she wished Julian were here to talk it over.

She checked her phone and saw he'd left a text saying that he was going to see Zapata and would join her later for the horseback riding lesson. She rubbed her eyes and read it again. Zapata? The man who was in tight with a Colombian cartel? The mastermind of Lorenzo's businesses? The vindictive monster who sent Damien to kill the Baker? If she hadn't been edgy before, Julian's morning agenda—which he should have discussed with her—was enough to start her adrenaline running.

What had happened to Angie the Loner? For the first time in her career with the FBI, she felt like she needed a partner, needed Julian. Though she wanted to call him or send a screaming text in all caps, she worried that someone might be listening to their communications. Reverting to her undercover role as his lover, she sent a big fat juicy heart emoji.

Her day was underway. Dressed for her riding lesson in a pair of purple Frye boots that matched a cowgirl shirt with an embroidered yoke, she took the elevator down to the OTB lounge on the lower level. Her office was behind the public area that was basically a tavern furnished with horsey memorabilia and big-screen TVs to watch every aspect of horse racing. She tapped in the code to unlock her office door, sidled inside and settled behind her long desk where a gang of computers were performing or waiting to be called upon. She waved at the screens, some of which were blank while others displayed constantly updated records of betting activity.

"Hello, boys." Her mouth stretched in a smile. "Did you miss me?"

Some people might think it was sad that her best friends were computers, but she liked her machines. If she entered the right program, a computer never betrayed her trust. When she wanted to play, they offered gazillions of games. And if she just wanted to sit quietly with her thoughts, they wouldn't interrupt.

The only facet of her life that a computer couldn't satisfy was the one that Julian had activated when he kissed her.

Last night, their time together left her yearning for more. After her steamy shower, she'd dressed in a satin chemise with no panties and arranged herself on the bed, prepared to greet him with everything she had. Instead, she'd given in to exhaustion and fallen asleep.

There was a knock on the office door. "Who is it?"

"It's Tamara. I have caffeine."

Angie opened the door. "You guessed the magic word."

Tamara held a tray from room service. "Do you want it out here or in there?"

Angie glanced at her friendly computers and decided not to put their beautiful circuitry in danger of a spill. "I'm pretty sure there won't be a crowd in the lounge. Monday morning at ten isn't exactly a busy time for horse races."

In the lounge, Tamara set the tray on a vacant table. "I used to go to the racetrack with my dad when I was a kid. The horses were beautiful. Dad let me stand at the railing so I could get a closer look when they'd prance around the track. Then we'd go to the clubhouse, which had a really cool vibe if you didn't mind the stink of cigarette smoke. Do you prefer coffee or tea?"

"Coffee without cream or sugar."

"That was my first guess, but I brought a latte and

hot water just in case." She lifted the domed plate cover to reveal scrambled eggs, bacon and hash browns. "Mind if I join you?"

"Sit." It would have been rude to send her away, and Angie realized that the last time she'd eaten was when she had the chocolate cupcake from Valentino's. "Have you recovered from Saturday night?"

"I had a wonderful time. Thanks for helping me bust out of my shell."

"It's hard to resist the power of a red dress." She shoveled a bite of silky, delicious eggs into her mouth. "Leif couldn't take his eyes off you."

Tamara inadvertently glanced through the door from the OTB to the sports betting venue where Leif worked. "We have a date on Thursday night. Fingers crossed, I hope there will be more. Now, tell me all about you and Julian."

"It seems we have more in common than we realized." *A vast understatement!* "We connected."

"Look at you," Tamara said. "You're glowing."

"Am I?" Glowing and blushing hadn't been part of her undercover disguise. Pretending to be involved with Julian was going to be easy.

"You make a classy couple—him looking like a professor with his glasses and you with your gorgeousness."

Angie concentrated on devouring her breakfast. "There's not much high-profile horse racing on today's schedule. I'm going to take advantage of the downtime to have another riding lesson with Waylon."

"How's that going?"

"It's okay." She had gotten far enough that she could mount and sit astride without feeling like she was going to puke.

Two gray-haired duffers shuffled into the lounge and settled themselves at a table where they opened their copies of the *Daily Racing Form*. These two were regulars and came to Nick's every day.

"Bert and Ernie," Tamara said as she stood. "I'll get those two some coffee. What time does your bartender come in?"

"Eleven o'clock and thanks for taking care of my guys. It's lonely down here. I want more bettors who stick around and start bringing their friends."

She finished her breakfast, sat back and sipped excellent coffee while Tamara chatted with the gruff but oddly charming old guys. Angie didn't know much about racing or off-track betting and still didn't completely understand the codes and notes on the racing forms, but she liked the atmosphere. Everybody at Nick's was easygoing and friendly. This would have been a great place to work, except for the criminal element. Last night's eruption into violence was a reminder that Nick's was more than yummy room service and lightweight legal vices.

She returned to her office to deal with the computerized aspect of gambling, which was several times bigger than the in-house OTB. Most of the members of this gentlemen's club placed their wagers online. According to her stats, the recent legalization of sports betting in Colorado hadn't affected the cash flow at Nick's, probably because Lorenzo offered advances on bets…for an exorbitant interest rate.

While she worked, Angie lost herself in a world of numbers. Her undercover identity claimed she was a math genius. Not true, but she enjoyed computations, projections and algorithms. When she finally looked up from her computers, a couple of hours had passed. She yawned, stretched and wondered why she hadn't heard from Julian.

What had happened at Zapata's office? She'd been trained to imagine alternatives and contingencies, most of which were disasters. As her colleague, Julian needed to keep her informed. In his pose as her lover, his attitude definitely had to change. He had to portray a guy who was obsessed, besotted and crazy about her, had to act like he couldn't stand being apart from her.

When she checked her phone again, there were no other texts from him. Instead, she accessed the encrypted link with her handler at the FBI. Special Agent Hemming had left details about the autopsies which provided very little new information. Damien and one of the others had the triple *H* tattoo from the Colombian cartel. The third man had a tat of Roman numerals. MMXV stood for 2015, a year that held significance for a gang that had started in Denver and spread across the Southwest. The gang called themselves the Fifteen.

Why was Damien in touch with MMXV? Had he been planning a double cross, breaking away from the cartel and doing business with a local gang? She hated to see so many other dangerous people involved with the trafficking, but that was the way these schemes worked.

From studying Lorenzo's accounts and computer files that she had access to, she suspected that the service he provided was mostly logistical. Zapata would collect payment from the cartels and gangs that smuggled human cargo, whether it was kids, maids, sex workers or field hands. Zapata would arrange contacts and transportation which resulted in a second payment. Lorenzo was pivotal to the operation but—true to his expensive taste with original artwork and the fantastic Glass Palace—he kept his hands clean. She had questions, a lot of questions, and needed to find time to sit down with Julian and compare data.

When she emerged from her office, she counted six patrons in addition to Bert and Ernie who had moved closer to one of the big-screen TVs. Waylon had joined them and was giving a low-key lecture about how to tell which horse was a winner.

"You can read all the stats you want," Waylon said, "but there ain't no substitute for experience and instinct. I spent my whole life with horses, and I can take a look at the field for this race and tell you the result. Win, place and show."

Bert and Ernie didn't agree with the old cowboy. They had a complicated system with different colored markers that checked off various aspects on the racing form. Then they factored in the history of the horse, took a look at the breeder and trainer and jockey. Their bets were generally under fifty bucks.

"Our system works," one of them said as he took a swig from his coffee mug. "Angie, tell him. It works."

Reluctantly, she admitted, "I don't quite understand how they do it, but they get results. Last week, they did 18 percent better than the house, including a bet on a thirty-three-to-one long shot."

A commotion announced the arrival of Leif Farnsworth. He wasn't a big name in horse racing, but everybody knew the former quarterback from the Denver team. He shook hands all around before he got sucked into Bert and Ernie's conversation.

"I'm guessing y'all know the answer to this question," Waylon said. "What's the best way to pick a winner? Statistics or instinct?"

Leif shrugged. "I like to go with my gut."

"Instinct," Waylon said triumphantly.

Bert and Ernie scowled in unison. One of them asked, "How often are you right?"

"More often than I lose, but not by much."

"What are the signs?" Waylon asked. "When y'all go into a game, how do you know if you're going to win or lose?"

"I always start off thinking I'm a winner. If I thought I was going to lose or get sacked or fumble, I wouldn't leave the dressing room. I never want to screw up, but sometimes it just happens." Leif shook his head. "I calculate the variables and check my level of confidence, but there's no way to prepare for the unexpected."

Not a bad way to describe life or fate or even love. No matter how confident you felt or how many calculations pointed toward success, the unexpected could rear its ugly head and wipe out any plan. When Angie heard more people approaching the OTB lounge, she craned her neck, hoping to see Julian. No such luck! Strolling through the door were Calamity Jane, Muscleman Matt the concierge and Cara, who dodged through the tables and chairs to give Angie a hug. Right behind them was Tamara, who zoomed in on Leif.

On the big-screen TV, the horses paraded around the track, giving the crowd a last look and time to place their bets. In horse racing, it seemed to take forever to prepare for a race that lasted only a few minutes. While Waylon described the gait and the energy from one of the two-year-old fillies, she went to the bar and ordered another cup of coffee.

Looking up into the long mirror behind the liquor bottles at the back of the bar, she watched the growing crowd but was still detached from it. Cara bounced across the room and climbed up on a stool beside her. Though it wasn't appropriate or legal to have a child in an establishment that served liquor, Cara was safer here than most other locations at Nick's.

"Waylon is gonna let me ride with my mom," Cara said. "I told him I could handle my own horse, but he says I'm not big enough."

And why would you want *to?* "Riding with your mom will be fine. She grew up on a ranch."

"Yep." Cara nodded vigorously, and her ponytail bounced. "We're gonna visit for Christmas, and I'll get to do more riding."

While she chattered about a pony with black and white spots, Angie could hear the love in Cara's voice.

When she'd been a seven-year-old, there had been nothing or no one she cared about so deeply. Maybe if she'd had an animal companion, she wouldn't have been such a troublemaker. Marigold was the only person she'd ever trusted. And Marigold had left her.

She felt a warm hand at her waist, looked up into the mirror above the bar and saw Julian standing beside her. Tamara was right. Side by side, they were a classy couple. He dropped a light kiss on her forehead.

Cara chirped. "Hey, Julian, you gotta give me a kiss. I'm your girlfriend, too."

"Absolutely." He brushed a kiss on the top of her head and tugged at her ponytail. "Why is everybody sitting around here and drinking coffee?"

"Beats me," Angie said. "My lesson isn't until two."

He scanned the crowd. "Is everybody coming along?"

"I am." Cara's hand shot into the air.

Being accompanied by a crowd would hamper their ability to search for Gigi. This wasn't what Angie had intended. "Jane and Matt will also be joining us. And Tamara might have mentioned that she'd like to tag along."

"Why?" Julian asked.

"Checking out the gossip," Cara said with a flip of her ponytail. "They want to know if you two are boyfriend and girlfriend."

"I'll never tell." Julian checked his watch and leaned closer to her. "We're going to get a head start. Just you and me."

A good way to search without a mob! Though she liked his solution, she had a few doubts. "How much do you know about horses?"

"I grew up on a ranch in Wyoming. Is that good enough for you?"

"You're good enough for me," she said softly, "in every way."

"Yuck!" Cara shouted.

Chapter Sixteen

After a couple of quick excuses to the group in the OTB lounge, Julian took her hand and led her through the back hallways on the basement level.

"Where are we going?" she asked.

"This is part of the original structure before it was renovated into the gentlemen's club." He used a code on a keypad to open a door at the end of the hallway. When a green light gave the okay, they stepped through. "This was originally a root cellar."

"Cold and dank," she said. "That figures."

"No need to waste money keeping preserved peaches and salsa at the proper temperature. Not that there's any of that stuff down here anymore." The few bare bulbs shed a dim light. Even though it was the middle of the day, there was a creepy vibe. "Watch your step."

"A secret space," she said. "Nobody comes down here, which makes me think it might be perfect to use for—"

He silenced her with a kiss. Nuzzling her ear, he whispered, "We have to always act like somebody is watching and listening. And, yes, you're right. This is only one of many hidden places in Nick's that could be used for trafficking."

Before he was aware of what was happening, she went up on tiptoe to kiss his throat, then she caught his earlobe in her teeth. Her light nibbles sent electric fire along his nerve endings. "What kind of idiot," she whispered, "would put surveillance down here?"

"Not so dumb if they plan to use the area for storing human cargo."

She broke away from his embrace and announced to anyone who might be listening, "I was going to say that this would make a fantastic wine cellar."

"We already have a wine cellar, a big one."

When he opened the door on the opposite side of the former root cellar, they came out at the far end away from the loading dock. The bunkhouse was almost straight ahead, and the barn was across the driveway to the left. Weather in Colorado was unpredictable in October. In spite of the golden aspens, today felt more like springtime than the edge of winter.

Angie turned her face up to the sun. With her head tilted back, her long, platinum braid reached almost to her waist. He wanted to kiss her again…and then again. After spending the morning in the company of Zapata and Lorenzo, Julian needed some sweetness to erase the foul taste from his mouth. He hated to ruin the mood with the news about tomorrow night, but they had to start planning.

He ducked his head down and whispered in her ear as they strolled toward the barn. "I have important information."

"Which reminds me…you need boyfriend lessons. A lover doesn't send a vague text about visiting a super-villain and then disappear for hours. You need to tell me where you are, and it wouldn't hurt for you to use a heart emoji or two."

"I'm a guy. I can't do the smiley valentines."

"And don't be afraid to use the L-word." She smoothed her hair. "What did you learn from Zapata?"

He hedged, trying to ease into the bad news that they were running out of time. "The most important detail came from Lorenzo, who showed up just in time to keep me from throwing Rudy off the sixth floor terrace of the office building. That punk kid knew about Damien and didn't tell me. He and Zapata both refused to talk about the trafficking, wouldn't even admit that was the plan. Neither did Lorenzo but he said that an important project would be starting on Tuesday night. And he'll have his own men posted at the barn."

"Tuesday?" An audible gasp escaped her lips. "That's tomorrow."

"It could be a preliminary trial run or could be the real thing. Either way, we need to be ready."

They were almost to the barn when she came to a halt and rooted her little purple boots to the ground. "I can't believe what you just told me. What a disaster! In light of that, I'm not ready to get back on the horse."

"But I was going to help you. That was our excuse for coming out here."

"Make up a different excuse." She pivoted and marched toward the bunkhouse. "The real reason we're out here is to find Gigi. If something is happening tomorrow night, we need to get her somewhere safe."

At the corner of the bunkhouse, Angie turned uphill and hiked around to the back. The long, rugged one-story building was built after WWII at the same time as the original lodge. The structure was sturdy but not neatly finished. Angie opened a shutter to peek through a window.

"I can't see a thing," she said. "But this would be a good place for Gigi to hide if she could figure out how to get inside."

"So would the barn." Both would be good places for the traffickers. "Didn't Cara say that Gigi made a nest in one of the stalls?"

"That's right, but I'm discounting the barn because of the surveillance and other people coming and going. Cara also said she saw Gigi playing on this hillside."

"When was that?"

"Saturday."

"Before Saturday, when was the last time Cara saw Gigi?"

Angie paused and concentrated. "Two weeks ago and maybe some other times."

He considered it unlikely that a nine-year-old child with no special skills or knowledge of the area had managed to stay hidden for two weeks. Though the weather had been mild, the temperature dropped at night, sometimes into the twenties or lower. "If she's still around here, she must have found someplace warm to sleep."

"Like the bunkhouse." She tromped around to the

end where there was a stoop and a door. "I don't see a keypad. Do you have some secret way to enter?"

This ramshackle old building didn't rate special locks and devices. With no one living here, the bunkhouse wasn't worthy of special protection. He turned over a suspiciously smooth rock beside the stoop and took out the key that was tucked in a hidden compartment. "Not exactly high-tech."

"As long as it gets us inside," she said. "I hope we can find her. She'll be a good witness."

"Are you sure about that?" He fitted the key in the lock. "Most lawyers hate to use children as witnesses. They tend to be unpredictable and suggestible."

"True, but we need to put together evidence. Witness testimony is a good place to start. And I have access to another witness—someone who knows everything about Lorenzo."

"Marigold." He still wasn't one hundred percent sure about Angie's connection to her long-lost friend. He didn't think she was lying to him about Marigold, but she hadn't seen the woman in eleven years. Marigold could have changed. Angie had been nearly hysterical when they met. But Marigold was calm. He didn't trust her.

"She's coming here at six o'clock. If we meet in my room, I can make sure nobody is watching or listening."

"I'd like to sit in on that conversation."

"This is something I need to do alone."

She pushed open the door and entered the bunkhouse. The interior was plain and unadorned with a propane heater and stove at the front and five bunk beds on either side. He flicked the switch by the door and was surprised when the electricity came on. Had someone been using this place? Had Zapata turned on the electric in preparation for the human trafficking?

"The beds aren't made." She went to a closet and unfastened the latch to a walk-in space lined with shelves. "Everything is put away, nice and neat. Blankets, sheets, pillows and towels. If Gigi used any of these supplies, she did an amazing job of cleaning up after herself. There's not a wrinkle in sight."

At the other end of the bunkhouse were toilets and showers. When he turned faucets, no water came out, which was as it should be. In winter, they drained any water outlets that weren't in use so the pipes wouldn't freeze. "She didn't come in here to clean up."

"But it's close to the hotel where there are plenty of bathrooms. Gigi could have taken a blanket and towel from the bunkhouse."

"I think we're giving our nine-year-old fugitive too much credit," he said. "In a two-week period, someone would have noticed a little girl wandering around unsupervised. Nick's isn't a place where children are welcome."

"If she's not here, then where? At the bakery, Damien said they'd lost track of the little girl. That has to be Gigi."

Julian was torn. If a child had really gone missing, they had been treating the situation badly. There needed to be an Amber Alert, plus calls to the local police, the FBI and CBI. But Gigi might be part of Cara's imagination or one of the employees' kids. Dozens of explanations were credible. He wanted to believe there was nothing to worry about, but Damien and Valentino had referred to a missing child. "We need to talk to Cara."

"I should take a pass on that conversation," Angie said. "I don't usually like kids, but Cara is different. She's special. And I have a nasty suspicion that she's playing me."

"You? You're letting a seven-year-old get under your skin? I thought you were supposed to be tough and street smart."

"Maybe I'm turning mushy." She gave a quick, ironic laugh. "Isn't that what's supposed to happen to a woman in love?"

He couldn't let a comment like that slide on by. In a few strides, he crossed the bunkhouse and stood before her. "Are you hinting that I'm making you melt?"

"Like a sunlamp on ice cream." She reached up and took off his glasses. "You're a distraction. It's hard to be rational when I'm looking into those baby blue eyes."

"Good."

He snugged his arm around her waist and pulled her close. This time, when they kissed, he took his time to savor the flowery scent of her shampoo. He glided his fingers down her spine and caressed the flare of her hips. She was as perfect as a marble sculpture but better because she moved against him and made little moaning sounds in her throat. No one could see them in here. This kiss wasn't part of the show to make people think they were lovers. They were embracing because they wanted to be in each other's arms. He kissed her harder, imagined that he could feel her heartbeat becoming synchronized with his. They were becoming one.

When they separated, she rested her cheek against his chest. She was breathing heavily as though she'd run a marathon, and he was the same—tense from exertion and more tense from holding back. "Before the others get here," she said, "we ought to lock the door. There are ten different beds, and I think we can figure out how to use at least two or three of them."

"Not now." He wanted their first time to be more than an afternoon quickie. "Tonight after Marigold visits, I'll come to you."

"It's a good thing that one of us is rational." She took a reluctant step away from him. "I'm worried about seeing Marigold, don't know what to expect from her. I'm a little bit afraid. I don't want to be hurt."

"You don't have to face the pain alone."

From outside the bunkhouse, he heard the sound of the others approaching the barn. Cara's flutelike voice played counterpoint to Muscleman Matt's rumbling basso, and Jane added a steady note of calm. Waylon wasn't doing any of the talking, which wasn't surprising. The old cowboy generally kept his thoughts to himself.

Before he and Angie left the bunkhouse, Julian turned off the light and flipped the lock on the door. At the stoop, he stashed the key in the secret compartment of the fake rock—a hiding place worthy of a Scooby cartoon. In keeping with the kid show theme, he was about to interrogate a little girl about her imaginary friend. This morning's confrontation with Zapata and

Lorenzo felt like it took place on a darker, more dangerous planet where violence occurred on a regular basis. Julian had no one to blame but himself for the amusement park atmosphere at Nick's. He'd done his best to sanitize operations by turning strippers into performers and regulating the betting limits in the casino.

When they entered the barn, Cara stamped her little foot and scolded. "You guys were supposed to already be riding."

"My fault," Angie said. "It's such a pretty day. I just wanted to walk and enjoy the aspen gold."

Cara narrowed her gaze. "Maybe you were putting off your ride because you're scared."

"Maybe."

In his head, Julian changed her "maybe" to "definitely." Angie's complexion flushed, and her hand trembled. Being around horses wasn't easy for her. Gently, he suggested, "We could put this off for another day."

"I can do it." She faced Waylon. "Where do we start?"

"Y'all saddle up. Angie, you come with me. Matt and Jane, bring in three horses from the corral and get them ready to ride."

Cara counted on her fingers. "One for Mom and one for Matt and one for Julian. We need another horse for me."

"Not today, little one. You're riding with your mom."

When she stomped out the barn door, Julian followed. Cara stuffed her hands into the pockets of her jeans and scowled at the ground beneath her feet. At the corral, she peered through the railings and watched as her mom and Matt approached a chestnut mare with a black mane and tail. They worked together well, slipping a bridle on the mare and leading her into the barn.

Julian leaned against a fence post beside Cara. "Do you know why we came to the barn for a ride today?"

She nodded. "We're looking for Gigi."

"Angie mentioned that you saw her on Saturday. Any other times?"

"A couple of weeks ago," she said, "and once after that or maybe twice. I don't get to come up here much because I gotta stay in Denver and go to stupid old school. Science is okay, but I hate math."

Cara could babble all afternoon and not tell him anything he needed to know. Julian tried to focus her conversation. "Back to Gigi. Do you think she slept in the barn overnight?"

"I dunno." Her skinny shoulders rose and fell in a shrug. "The first time I saw her, she had a cozy little hideout in the straw inside one of the horse stalls. The next day I came back, and she wasn't there."

"Did you ask Waylon if he'd seen her?"

"Not right away."

She turned away from the corral and skipped over to a plain wooden bench. She hopped up on it and balanced as she tiptoed from one end to the other. He couldn't tell if she was avoiding his questions or just didn't care. "Did you tell your mom about Gigi?"

"Gigi is my friend, and she asked me not to tell anybody. If people found out she was here, she'd get in trouble because she was running away from home."

A runaway? That was new information. The elusive Gigi might not be part of a trafficking operation. She might be a kid running away from home. "Where's she running away from? Does she live up here in the mountains?"

"I dunno."

He wasn't going to get anywhere by threatening her, but his supply of patience was running low. "How about a last name?"

"I don't remember."

At times like this, his sobriety was tested. A shot of tequila might have made this conversation easier. "Maybe Gigi told you something about the people she lives with. Were there any other kids? Did she have a mom and a dad?"

"We didn't talk so much. We played."

"Think, Cara. It's important."

She jumped off the bench, folded her arms around her middle and scowled. "Are you mad at me?"

Expecting simple, direct answers from a seven-year-old was a long shot. He sat on the bench and forced a smile. "I'm not mad."

"Your voice sounds like you are."

"Come over here and sit next to me." He patted the bench. "I promise not to snap your head off."

Her gaze glued to his face as she took a seat on the bench. "Is Gigi in trouble?"

"I hope not." Counting to ten, he slowly exhaled. "Let's do this a different way, okay?"

"Sure."

"I like you, Cara, and I know you're a smart kid. Why don't you just tell me everything you remember about Gigi? The way she looks, her clothes, the games you played, everything."

"Here goes," she said. "Gigi is very pretty, has brown hair and her favorite color is red. The first time I saw her, her outfit was brown and gold. She had a little notebook and drew lots of pictures. I wanted her to give me a picture of a fairy princess, but she said she'd better not because she was running away and didn't want to leave clues. She was scared of a big man who smelled like doughnuts. He grabbed her and put her in a van with other people."

Julian wiped his hand across his mouth to keep himself from interrupting. This version of the story sounded more like Gigi had gotten swept up in a trafficking scheme.

Cara continued, "You probably don't believe in fairy princesses because you're a boy, but they're real and they protect kids like Gigi and me. Gigi's princess made sure she'd be warm at night and got food for her. So did I...bring her food. On Saturday when I saw her, I got a sandwich from the kitchen for her."

"Wait." He couldn't stay silent for one more second. "Are you telling me that you managed to sneak out from the concierge level?"

"It's not hard." She gave him a sly smile. "I could show you all the secret doors."

"You're amazing, kiddo."

"I know."

They both turned and watched as Angie rode from the barn. Her posture was as rigid as the stripper pole in the Burlesque, and she bounced straight up and down in the saddle. Though her horse walked slowly, she pulled on the reins and jammed her right foot down as if she was stomping on a brake.

Beside him, Cara snickered. “Your girlfriend looks dopey.”

“It doesn’t change the way I feel about her.”

And that, he realized, might be the closest he’d ever come to a declaration of love.

Chapter Seventeen

Julian's penthouse suite on the seventh floor was decorated in earth tones and a southwestern motif similar to the rest of the hotel but with an elevated level of style. Everything was bigger: the floor space, the sofa and the TV. The walls were hung with modern artwork, and the shelves held a variety of handmade Native American pottery. Angie strolled past the fireplace to a wall of windows with a sliding panel that opened onto a wide balcony overlooking hills and forest. She pushed the door open and stepped into a soft gray dusk that smelled of pine and smoke from the barbecue outside the kitchen. The peaceful atmosphere seemed like an unlikely location for the heinous crime of human trafficking.

Stepping around the circular breakfast table, she went to the railing. He joined her and placed a ceramic coffee mug in her hand. She wanted to believe that the FBI and CBI would shut down the trafficking operation on Tuesday night, and no one would be hurt.

"You know," she said, "this balcony would be a great place for a hot tub."

He tapped his mug against hers. "Too bad I won't be living here long enough to justify the trouble and expense of installing one. There are a lot of things I would have done differently if this was going to be my permanent home."

"Like what? The art and the pottery are beautiful."

"The decor is great, but it's not mine. I like that painting with the sand dunes and the cow skull, but I don't have any personal stories about how I found an artist in Santa Fe who studied with Georgia O'Keeffe. The pottery and woven baskets came with the place. You might be interested to know that your friend Marigold, in her identity as Marian, was the decorator."

"Not surprised, she always was artistic." Angie checked her watch with the tooled leather band. Marigold was scheduled to meet with her in less than two hours in her suite on the fourth floor. If she was ready to leave Lorenzo, Angie could make that happen. Marigold would be first in line for a new life as a protected witness. On the other hand, if she didn't want to separate from the scumbag who took advantage of her when she was a teenager, the situation could turn complicated. Angie didn't want to see Marigold swept up with the other thugs. Could she arrange for her friend to escape?

Julian draped an arm around her shoulder and pulled her close. His natural aroma mingled with the scent of the forest. She leaned against his shoulder, enjoying their closeness and wishing it could last for longer than a day.

"You're tense," he said.

"I don't know if Marigold will want to say goodbye

to her sweet lifestyle in the Glass Palace. How can she walk away from a closet full of designer clothes and jewelry? And all that money…it's real seductive."

"Whoever said crime doesn't pay hasn't been hanging out with the right criminals."

"You get it." She tilted her head so she could look up at his profile. "When this is over, you're going to hate leaving Nick's."

"Damn right I am! I like having room service and maid service and valets to fetch my car whenever I want. I like the money. Most especially, I've liked being able to build this place and organize the operations. Best job I've ever had, and that includes being an agent for the CBI."

As soon as he mentioned being an agent, her senses went on high alert. "Is it safe to talk about the CBI?"

"A hundred percent safe. When we're in the penthouse, nobody can hear us or watch what we're doing. It's one of the perks I get for being in charge of security and surveillance. Plus I've constructed firewalls and other protections." He glanced over his shoulder at the interior. "We should go inside and make our contact with your handler and SSA Shanahan."

"I got a text from Hemming about the autopsy results. He mentioned a tattoo on one of Damien's friends. Roman numerals, MMXV."

"A Denver-based gang. They're bad news. I knew they were connected with Lorenzo."

When she turned in his arms and faced him, she was momentarily distracted by the scruff that roughened his jaw and the fire in his eyes. Even in the dusk, that incredible blue shone like a laser. She dragged her focus back to their work. "How do you know about the MMXV gang?"

"You know how much I hate being watched all the time."

"So do I."

"But I love being able to see everybody else. Do you remember the first night you were here and we ran into Lorenzo in the lobby?"

She shuddered and set her coffee on the table so she wouldn't slop it all over her bedazzled jeans. "Unforgettable."

"He was having a dinner meeting with a politician, which my surveillance cameras recorded. I couldn't get clear audio from the table where he was sitting, but a hidden mic picked up a few phrases. I transmitted all of it to SSA Shanahan."

"I'm guessing that you've taken video and audio of Lorenzo and Zapata with other of their cronies, including the boss from MMXV, the Fifteen."

"The boss who refers to himself as El Jefe, plus the head of the Colombian cartel that Damien worked for. I've recorded them all—from the hotshot bosses in solid gold chains and five-thousand-dollar suits to the snakeheads and coyotes covered in desert dust. When Lorenzo goes down, he'll take a network of other traffickers with him."

"Respect," she said. "I can understand why the CBI kept you here for three years."

He glided his hand down her cheek and cupped her chin. "I'd like to claim that I planned the whole undercover setup, but it was mostly luck. I happened to be in the right place at the right time to meet Lorenzo, and we clicked."

"It took more than luck to keep this operation running. Don't deny it, Professor. You're a smart cookie."

"Gotta live up to my reputation."

Quick and hot, his mouth pressed against hers. It was like being kissed by a flame. Then he escorted her through the front room to an office where he opened a hinged painting of cowboys on horseback. Behind the painting was a wall safe and inside that was a computer. He wasn't joking when he talked about the layers of protection.

He set up the laptop on his desk and, with a few strokes on the keyboard, enabled a conference chat with Hemming and Shanahan. The two agents were waiting for their call in a bland conference room—could have been CBI or FBI—with documents, maps and photos spread across the table. Her least favorite part of the job was reporting and paperwork, and she was glad to see that Julian was cool with handling those duties.

With very little participation from her, the three men discussed a plan of action for Tuesday night when Lorenzo had guards posted at the barn. Julian had sent maps of possible places where human cargo could be off-loaded and held until final destinations were arranged. The tricky part would be to rescue the people being trafficked without having anyone get hurt. Very likely, there would be frightened children and young women.

"How can I help?" she asked.

Hemming frowned at the screen. "Me and Shanahan, we talked this over and decided that both of you should maintain your undercover identities as long as possible. We've got teams of experienced field agents who are familiar with procedures for rescue and extraction missions. You and Julian lay low."

"No problem." Angie was happy to let the experts take charge. "Will you be making simultaneous arrests at different locations?"

"We'll pick up Lorenzo and Zapata," Hemming said. "Are you worried about your friend Marigold?"

"Who's Marigold?" Shanahan asked.

"You probably know her as Marion Grant, Lorenzo's mistress," Hemming explained. "Angie knew her when they were both teenagers. They were close."

"And I don't want her to be arrested," Angie said. "She's a good person who got caught up with bad people. I can get her to testify against Lorenzo."

"We'll do what we can," Shanahan promised, "but I'm afraid your friend might be implicated in some of Lorenzo's personal financial documents. By the way, you did an excellent job gathering that information."

"It was easy. They handed over the paperwork and codes so I could revamp their OTB operations."

"Between your documents and Julian's surveillance, we have a good start to our case against these guys. Picking up eye witnesses to the trafficking operation should seal the deal."

In less than an hour, Angie would have a chance to talk to Marigold and convince her to step away from Lorenzo. She had to make that happen.

"One more thing," Julian said. "A little girl named Gigi might be caught up in all this. If we can find her, she'd make a good witness."

"A missing child," Hemmings said. "Are we talking about a kidnapping? Why is this the first I'm hearing about it?"

"It's complicated." Angie tried to explain. "The only person who has seen Gigi is a seven-year-old who might have exaggerated the situation. But I agree with Julian. We need to keep looking for her."

SSA Shanahan nodded. "Let us know how we can help."

After more of a discussion about strategy, their conference was over. Julian closed the screen and returned the laptop to the safe above his desk. "I managed to pry a few more details from Cara this afternoon."

"Was that before or after you were both laughing at me?"

For a moment, he seemed to be studying her, assessing her possible reaction. Then he shook his head and grinned. "Nope, I can't deny that we were making fun of you. I never thought anyone could look so uncomfortable on horseback."

"People get killed in riding accidents." She knew for a fact that horses were dangerous creatures. "There are serious injuries."

"Not when the horse is walking slower than a turtle."

With a flick of her wrist, she wiped away his comment. "Tell me about Cara."

"She told me that Gigi likes to draw, and she has a

fairy princess who brings her food and makes sure she has somewhere warm to sleep."

"A fairy princess, eh?" She cocked her head to one side. "A lot of women around here might fit that description. Every performer at the Burlesque is pretty and glittery enough to be a princess, and then there are maids, servers, cocktail waitresses and staff, even Tamara."

"You're saying that all women are princesses."

"Maybe they are. Tomorrow, we can ask around. One of these princesses might help us find Gigi."

"We're making progress," he said.

"Thank goodness I don't need to have those profit figures ready for Zapata until Thursday."

"Whoa." He took a step back and regarded her critically. "You do realize that you don't really work here, don't you?"

"Sometimes the lines get blurred. Has that happened to you?"

"More than once," he admitted.

"Like when Shanahan suggested that we act the part of lovers. That role fits."

"Undercover lovers," he murmured.

There was no reason to be embarrassed, but she felt a blush warming her cheeks. If they only had a few hours together, she needed to take advantage of this time with him and tell him about her feelings. *Honest feelings?* Since when had she been compelled to speak the truth?

"What is it, Angie?"

"After Marigold leaves, I want to come back here to your suite." In spite of her newfound dedication to honesty, she couldn't bring herself to say exactly what she meant: *I want to spend the night in your bed.*

"I'll be waiting."

The heat from his azure eyes told her that he understood what she really meant.

Chapter Eighteen

Marigold was late. Typical! She hadn't changed a bit. Punctuality hadn't been her thing when they were teenagers and still wasn't important to her. Phone in hand, Angie paced back and forth on the carpet in front of the sofa in her concierge-level suite. She paused to stare at the app-filled screen on her phone, hoping to see a text message, but there was nothing. Marigold had always been the cool one.

Angie's fingers poised over the keys. She could send her own message but didn't want to betray her excitement or anxiety. What if Marigold didn't come? Or refused to listen? So many things could go wrong.

In the small kitchenette, she opened the fridge under the counter beside the sink. The ice-cold craft beer was tempting, but she had the feeling that she needed all her wits to deal with her old friend. She grabbed a carton of cranberry juice, climbed onto a stool at the black granite counter that divided the kitchenette from the living room and helped herself to the white chocolate and macadamia nut cookies that were provided free, compliments of room service.

Probably not a good idea to cram a cookie into her mouth, but she took two anyway. The amenities at Nick's were outstanding, and she might not have this level of service for a very long time. Her next under-cover assignment might not be luxurious, but that wasn't the reason she wanted to stay here. In spite of the dan-ger, deception and horseback riding lessons, Nick's felt like home. She'd met people here who were already like family…and Julian, her undercover lover. How could she leave before she had a chance to find out if their budding relationship might bloom.

She checked the time on her phone. Marigold was of-ficially twenty-three minutes late. Swell! She polished off the cookie and brushed the crumbs off her crimson, high-collared blouse with the low V-neck to show off her necklaces of crystals and silver. When it was half an hour, Angie would call.

There was a tap at the door, and she flew to answer. The blonde woman who pushed her way inside with-out being invited smelled like expensive perfume. Her makeup was perfect. Her short, faux fur, leopard-print jacket over super-skinny jeans would have been tacky on a less confident woman, but Marigold made them look fashionable. She glanced around the room as if she owned the place.

"You decorated this suite," Angie said.

"I'm good at my work."

"Are you an interior decorator by trade?"

"I've had some training, and I have good taste, which is as much of a shock to me as anybody else."

"I always knew you were tasteful. You used to read

all the fashion mags." Their conversation seemed as stilted as two people who had never met before. Angie wanted to dash across the room and give her oldest pal—perhaps her only true friend—a hug. "I missed you."

"Same here."

"I never thought I'd see you again."

"When I look back at who we were when we were teenagers, I wouldn't have given good odds for our survival."

"We did okay. With no cash and no skills, we got by for six months on the road."

"Don't make it sound like we were on a grand adventure. I was there. I remember the days when we had nothing to eat but the crap we scrounged from dumpsters. My back still aches from the nights when we slept under streetlights on concrete."

Angie tended to gloss over the horror of that time when they'd meandered from Utah to Denver. They'd taken turns saving each other's life. The predators were many and fierce. Running from a massive brown bear in the forest was less terrifying than facing street gangs in the city. "I never would have made it without you."

"Me? What about you? You were ferocious, especially after you bought your first switchblade at that weird little pawnshop."

"I've upgraded since then."

"Smart move. That first blade was clumsy and ridiculous. The only thing it was good for was scaring off somebody who got too close."

"Not our best weapon," she conceded. "You were better at disarming men."

"Like this." Marigold opened her leopard jacket. Underneath the faux fur, she wore a snug, cream-colored top that revealed her shapely, well-toned body. "A blessing and a curse."

She did a little shimmy, and Angie laughed. "You've always been gorgeous."

"And you were the smarty-pants."

Angie felt herself beginning to relax. At the Glass Palace when she'd first seen the woman who called herself Marion Grant, she'd been too shocked and confused to do anything more than dissolve into a helpless puddle of tears. The last couple of days had given her perspective. "You said you were willing to leave Nick."

"I say a lot of things." She stalked across the room and came to a stop only a few feet away. "You're calling yourself Angie, right?"

"I've used a dozen aliases since I was fifteen. I'm sure you've done the same because I've continued to look for you online over the years, and 'Marion Grant' doesn't exist. I followed a number of false trails that all led to dead ends. You're the most secret of mistresses with no identification whatsoever."

"Aren't you clever?" Standing too close, she flicked the collar of Angie's red shirt. "Tell me, Angie, are you wearing a wire?"

"Of course not. Why would your think that?"

"You've been looking for me, and this afternoon I did some research of my own. The usual computer stuff was all about your alias, and there was nothing on the name I once knew you by. Do you even remember being Maxine Dubrowski?"

Maxie and Marigold. Before they teamed up, she'd been a sullen brat who kept to herself and lashed out at the well-meaning adults who tried to take care of her. Living with her drug-addict parents would have been worse, but she could never forgive them for abandoning her. She didn't thrive in foster care, didn't have a sense of herself at all until she hooked up with Marigold. "What did you find out?"

"I called a couple of the homes where we lived. One of the foster moms—a tall woman with a faint mustache—told me that you were a success story and had turned your life around."

"And Mrs. Mustache probably claimed credit, told you that I had seen the error of my ways and become a good girl."

"It wasn't really like that."

Angie had no particular aspiration to be a good girl. Instead, her motivation for doing well in school and developing a power base was simple. She wanted revenge against Lorenzo for taking Marigold away from her. "What else did she tell you?"

"She said you'd gone to college, graduated and then went into law enforcement. Is that accurate? Are you a cop?"

Marigold locked her gaze on Angie's face. This was it: the moment of truth.

Though they had been apart for eleven years, Marigold was closer to her than anyone else. They were sisters. Lying to her was an unthinkable betrayal. Angie knew she could pull off a deception. Based on her psychological profile and her FBI training in undercover work, she was a certified, world-class liar.

And she had a solid basis for concealing the truth. Like it or not, Marigold had been Lorenzo's mistress for over eleven years. If Angie gave up the details of the FBI raid on Tuesday night, his mistress might feel obliged to tell him, and the plan to halt human trafficking would fail. Three years of undercover work by Julian would be wasted, not to mention her own elaborate subterfuge and research.

Angie stuck out her chin. "I'm not wearing a wire. Are you?"

"What?"

"If you really think I'm a cop, you might have wanted to record our conversation for Lorenzo. And before you say anything else, I want you to know that all the recording devices—audio and cameras—have been disabled in my suite."

"Does your boyfriend know about that?"

"I convinced Julian that I needed my privacy."

Marigold took a step back. "I heard that you hooked up with him. I totally approve. I worked with Julian when I was decorating, and I like the guy. He's smart, practical and has the prettiest blue eyes of all time. Don't let him get away."

Relationship advice from a woman who hooked up with a crime boss? "I might not stay on the OTB job too long."

"Why would you leave?"

"I don't like horses. Once I get the initial computer

system up and running, there won't be much more for me to do." So far, she'd been honest. "I'm not crazy about Valentino, and Zapata scares me."

"Where would you go?"

"I have options." She clasped Marigold's hands in both of hers. "And so do you. You said you were tired of Lorenzo, and I can help you get away from him and start a new life. You're beautiful and talented. You deserve good friends and a family who loves you as much as I do. Come with me, Marigold, you always said you wanted kids."

Her gaze flickered, and Angie knew she'd hit a sore point. Was this about children? Was Marigold desperate to have kids? She stalked across the room to the door and paused with her hand on the knob. "I'll be in touch."

"Don't leave."

"I can't stay. I need to get home."

"Promise you'll call me or come over tomorrow," Angie pleaded. "Promise."

"I'll try."

She whipped open the door and exited.

In Julian's penthouse suite, Angie prowled the room like a hungry mountain lion searching for prey. Her meeting with Marigold hadn't been satisfying. The big question about whether she'd leave Lorenzo remained unanswered, and Angie sensed that her friend was troubled in many other ways.

"Anything to drink?" Julian asked. "I have wine, beer, juice, lemonade and tea."

"Why do you keep booze in the house if you don't drink?"

"It's for guests. And the craft beer is nonalcoholic."

"I'll try that." She climbed onto a high stool and rested her elbows on the granite counter that separated his kitchenette. Though the rest of his suite was much bigger than hers, his cooking area was only slightly larger and contained a full-size fridge. "I've never been much of a drinker," she said. "I hate being drunk and out of control."

"Did your parents drink?"

"I didn't know them well enough to talk about their habits. They were both addicts, so I guess they drank, snorted and shot up. I'm lucky I didn't inherit those traits."

As he took two bottles of beer from the fridge and poured the contents into pilsner glasses, she appreciated his efficiency and economy of motion. He wasn't one of those guys who fumbled in the kitchen and couldn't take care of himself. When he pushed up the sleeves on his black cashmere sweater, she admired his muscular wrists. This was a man, a real man, who knew how to build a house, program a computer and make dinner.

"I bet you like to cook," she said.

"Sometimes. How about you?"

"Never," she said.

He brought the beer to the counter and leaned across to place her drink directly in front of her. Behind his glasses, his magical blue eyes ignited fireworks inside her. "Tell me about Marigold."

"It's hard to explain." She took a moment to compose herself and sip the craft beer, which had a smooth, wheaty flavor and tickled the back of her throat. "I couldn't bring myself to lie to Marigold, but I wasn't honest. She'd done background checking on me and asked if I was wearing a wire. She thought I'd become a cop."

"Which you didn't. You're an agent."

"I knew you'd say that." She noticed that he'd shaved while she'd been downstairs talking to her old friend. His dark blond hair was still damp from his shower. "You and I are very much alike when it comes to undercover work and deception. We're professional liars."

"Somehow, we managed to spend several days together without revealing our identities. Was anything you told me the truth?"

"Some of it."

"What's your real name?"

"Maxine Dubrowski," she said without hesitation. "I prefer Angie."

"Good to know," he said. "On the day after tomorrow, this assignment will be over and we'll go our separate ways and find new undercover identities."

She was well aware that the end was near. Their relationship would be over before it started. "We may never see each other again."

He glanced toward the fridge. "Hungry?"

"You did a good job of pretending to be dangerous. When you first drove me into the mountains, I halfway expected to be disappeared and dumped in a shallow grave. And when you loaded three dead guys in the back of the SUV, I was justifiably terrified."

"I didn't have a clue that you were FBI." He took a drink and licked the foam from his lips. "When I first met you, I almost broke my cover. You seemed like a decent person and—"

"Decent person? That's what you thought of me?"

"It's a compliment. I wanted to get you away from here and didn't want you to be hurt. Is that so terrible?"

"Not terrible but irritating." She wasn't ready to let him off the hook. "I go to a lot of trouble to look like this. Most men are fascinated and intrigued."

"If I fell apart every time I caught a glimpse of cleavage and a smear of red lipstick, there's no way I could work at the Burlesque." He scooped up their beer glasses and crossed the room. "Let's sit over here and get comfortable."

She followed him to the love seat in front of the fireplace. He set their drinks on the coffee table, dimmed the lights and lit the fire with the touch of a button. The flames scampered across the logs in a random dance that captivated her attention, but she noticed when he added background music—classical guitar. Comfy? Yes! Relaxed? Most definitely not. Her senses were on high alert. Her pulse raced.

The love seat was just the right size for cuddling. When he sat beside her, it would have been natural to slide into an embrace. She resisted, perching on the edge of the love seat and tasting her beer. "Are you sure this stuff isn't alcoholic? I'm feeling light-headed."

"That was my plan."

"This seduction scene isn't necessary," she said. "I

wouldn't have come to your suite if I hadn't intended to take our friendship to the next level."

"Friendship?" It was his turn to be insulted. "After we kissed? Last night, we slept together."

"And nothing happened. We didn't make love."

An echo of the L-word hung in the air between them. She set her glass on the table and reclined on the small sofa with his arm draped around her. She didn't usually think of sex as "making love." Why had she used that phrase with him? Loving him would be crazy.

Her thoughts returned to her conversation with Marigold. "When you said you wanted to protect me and make sure I wasn't hurt, that's exactly how I feel about my friend. I want to tell her that I'm FBI and can get her into witness protection."

"But you can't compromise the assignment," he said. "The stakes are high. If we fail to break up this trafficking operation, hundreds of lives will be destroyed. I know we're not saving the world, and someone else will fill in the gap left by Lorenzo, but I believe we can make a difference."

"That's why I didn't break cover."

He smoothed the hair off her forehead and stroked her long, smooth ponytail. "Last night when you collapsed in the bed, you unfastened your hair. Can I do that now?"

"Me, first."

She stroked his granite jawline. With both hands, she removed his glasses and put them on the coffee table. Making direct eye contact, she leaned closer and closer until she could smell the woodsy scent of his aftershave.

Her mouth joined with his. Of course, their kiss was a perfect fit. They were mirror images of each other—alike in so many ways and yet different.

He spun her around so her back was to him, and he unfastened her ponytail. His fingers combed through her long hair and pulled the sleek, platinum blond strands into a coil. He rotated her head so she was facing him. His kiss wasn't sweet or gentle. He was demanding, which was exactly what she wanted from him.

She had rough desires of her own. Gathering handfuls of black cashmere, she yanked his sweater and T-shirt over his head. His bared chest pressed hard against her, and he unfastened her red shirt with more finesse than she'd used.

The love seat was too small to contain their passion. He lifted her in his arms and carried her toward the bedroom. They didn't make it that far.

She didn't want to be handled like a child. If she could have thrown him over her shoulder in a fireman's carry, she would have. Angie swung her legs down and staggered back, bumping against the dining table.

Her plan had not included lying back on the table like an entrée, but she didn't object when he slowly, carefully devoured her. He kissed and caressed his way down from her throat to her breasts and lower. Heat blasted through her and torched her inhibitions. She wanted more of him—all of him. She wanted him inside her. And that was no lie.

In the bedroom, they tore off the rest of their clothes. Classical guitar thrummed in the background. Dim light from a bedside lamp outlined his lean, muscular body.

She jumped onto the bed and pointed at him. "Stay right there."

"Why?"

"It's been a long time," she admitted. "I want to look at you."

Though she'd intended to slowly memorize his wide-spread shoulders, the pattern of his chest hair and his flat belly, her gaze hopped from one feature to another like a sex-starved jackrabbit.

He flexed like a bodybuilder. "How's that?"

"Get over here, stud."

She reveled in their kisses and touches. This was sex—wild, raw and wonderful. But she couldn't help feeling that they were making love.

Chapter Nineteen

The next morning, Julian wakened slowly with memories of the night before stirring his blood. His mood elevated to a natural high. For a moment, he had a craving for vodka in his orange juice. Then his rational brain kicked in and reminded him that he was an alcoholic and couldn't drink, which was why he felt good and not hungover.

Reality landed with a thud. Today was going to be difficult and the bust tonight would be worse—filled with details and potential disasters. He started with the easy stuff: arranging rooms for SSA Shanahan and SA Hemming so they could stay on top of the action. He needed to start a search for the so-called "princess" who could lead him to Gigi. And then he could deal with the complex issue of the woman who was lying in bed beside him with her long hair rippling across the pillow. What should he do about Angie?

He watched her sleep, lying on her back with her arms thrown carelessly over her head. Her breasts and torso were covered by the sheet, but one of her long, firm legs had kicked free. She flexed her leg and pointed her toe emphasizing her muscular calf and the high arch on her foot.

He caught a piece of hair between his fingers and twirled the silky, platinum strand. God, she was beautiful! He had no idea what her other undercover disguises were like, but he knew this was his favorite. Not that he was usually drawn to sassy blondes with dramatic makeup and sparkly clothes. Julian had always liked natural, outdoorsy women. Why her? She looked ridiculous on horseback, and didn't wear shoes that were suitable for hiking. All things considered, she wasn't his type.

But when they were together, he felt fulfilled. He hated being apart from her. And the sex—the lovemaking—was magnificent. He gave a little tug on her hair. There was time this morning for another round.

She rolled away, made a quick grab for the bedside table and turned back toward him with her custom-made switchblade in her hand. Staring directly into his eyes, she pushed the button and the silver blade snicked open.

"I get it," he said. "You're not a morning person."

She closed the knife. "I'm taking a shower. In five minutes, you're invited to join me."

He watched her smooth back and naked bottom as she strode across the carpet into the adjoining bathroom. If he hadn't already been hard, that vision would have done it for him. He'd never expected her to pull a knife on him. When had she gotten the blade from the secret pocket in her jeans? Why did she feel the need to stash a weapon in the bedside table? Not that he had room to talk, there was a secret panel in his headboard where he kept a loaded gun.

He waited until he heard the water running to step into his bathroom. Julian hadn't gone to the expense of installing a hot tub on his balcony, but he'd splurged on a shower sauna with eight pulsating jets. The huge walk-in shower reminded him of a car wash. He could stand in the middle and get sprayed clean from all directions. Watching Angie through the glass walls of the shower was great. When he entered the enclosure, the view was even better. Steam billowed around their slick, wet bodies.

She slid her torso against his. "I wouldn't have stabbed you."

"Do you always sleep with a weapon?"

"Do you?" She chuckled. "I found the secret panel in your headboard."

He nodded. "Maybe we're too much alike."

Her upturned face, devoid of makeup, was beautiful and fresh. He pressed his mouth against hers and then nibbled her earlobe before trailing kisses down her throat to her breasts. Her body was perfect. As he made love to her, the inside of his brain exploded, and he was incapable of rational thought. His actions were driven purely by sensation and emotion.

Too soon, the sexy part of their shower was done. She clung to him and whispered, "I wish we had more time."

"We can squeeze in another hour or so."

"More time to be together," she said. "Our assignment will be over tonight, and I don't want to leave."

"Neither do I." When his time at Nick's was over,

he wouldn't be useful to the Colorado Bureau of Investigation as an undercover operative. Too many people knew him as Julian Parisi. His life would take a radical change.

She stepped from the shower and wrapped herself in a huge, fluffy towel—another extravagance. He wondered if he could take the towels with him when he left Nick's. Probably not, they might be considered evidence.

While Angie got ready to face the day, he ordered coffee and breakfast from room service. He was finished with the food and starting his second cup when she emerged from the bedroom wearing a black-and-white zebra patterned poncho over skinny black jeans and platform shoes that he knew had a spring-loaded compartment for a one-shot gun.

He looked her up and down. "Not exactly trying to fade into the woodwork, are you?"

"Oh, but I am. The poncho is reversible, and the other side is black. I switch it around and I'm invisible." She grabbed her coffee and downed half of it in one gulp. "What's the plan for today?"

"I need to arrange rooms for our bosses on a low floor with a clear view of the barn. I'm sure they'll have some issues to discuss, and I need to talk to them about making sure the people who work here will be safe during the bust."

"I wondered about that." She lifted the silver dome that covered her breakfast and made happy sounds about the bacon and eggs. "There are innocent people working here. You don't want them to get in the way if bullets are flying."

He had considered cutting back to a skeleton crew or coming up with a story about necessary repairs that meant his employees had to take a few days off. But he didn't want to do anything that might spook Lorenzo and Zapata. "The daily operations need to look normal."

She bit into her bacon and moaned with pleasure. "How about me? What should I do?"

"Aren't you supposed to be preparing a report for Zapata?"

"It's not due until Thursday," she said. "By then, everything ought to be shut down."

"But you're not supposed to know that. Zapata has people everywhere, watching you and reporting back to him."

"You're suggesting that I should fake doing the work." She shrugged. "I can pull that off. I'm good at faking it."

"I'll bet you are."

Angie raised her eyebrows, a smile slowly spreading from one side of her mouth to the other. "Here's a question," she said. "I know how I build my skills at deception. Growing up in foster care was risky. I needed to tell lies to survive. How did you learn?"

"According to the shrinks, I have a natural leaning in that direction that goes along with being an alcoholic. I started drinking when I was fourteen which meant I had to lie to my parents and teachers. When I got older, I hid my alcoholism from my employers, my friends and girlfriends. I'm ashamed to say that I got good at deceiving everybody."

"Everybody except yourself."

Her quick, accurate wisdom didn't surprise him. She was six years younger than him but had lived hard and crammed a lot of experience into her life. "You get me."

"I do," she said. "In addition to faking OTB statistics, what else can I do?"

"We need to find Gigi's princess."

AFTER AN EARLY LUNCH, Julian went downstairs to grab Angie and start their princess quest. On the way, he stopped in at the sports betting venue where Leif hunched over a beer and scowled at a hamburger. The handful of other people in the place ignored him, which seemed odd because the former quarterback was a local hero with adoring fans.

Julian pulled up a chair at Leif's table. "Something wrong?"

"Do you live under a rock? It's Tuesday, the day after *Monday Night Football*."

Julian guessed that the Broncos had played and lost. In this part of Colorado, that was reason for mourning. "Sorry."

"They gave up fourteen points in the fourth quarter. I was hosting a party here, and I got so ticked off that I had to leave before I punted one of those yahoos into next week."

Leif had a dark side. "I hope your day gets better, man. Have you seen Tamara?"

"Not today."

He left the sports venue and went to Angie's office. When he entered, she was playing a video game. She swiveled her chair, leaped from it and threw herself into his arms for a big, juicy kiss. He left the door wide-open, giving a view to the old duffers who bet on all the races. No big deal. He and Angie were undercover lovers, and it didn't matter who knew about their affair.

She whispered in his ear. "I got an encoded text message from Hemming. There's been unusual activity inside the gang that calls themselves the Fifteen. He's not sure what that means, but he and Shanahan are coming here early."

"How early?"

"He'd try to make it by two."

That only left an hour to debug their rooms and disable the cams. First, he wanted to interview the potential princesses who worked in the Burlesque. "Come with me. We should talk to Tamara, even though I don't really see her as Gigi's princess."

"Because she's not sparkly?" Angie gave a snort. "Rhinestones don't make a princess. Haven't you heard of Cinderella?"

He didn't bother to cite his appreciation for Tamara's inner beauty, her intelligence and her wit. It seemed like Gigi would call her princess based on clothes alone. At the front desk, he asked Tamara if Shanahan and Hemming—who were, of course, using fake names—had checked in.

"Not yet." Her forehead pinched in a frown. "Have you talked to Leif today?"

"He's sad. The Broncos lost." If that was the worst

thing that happened today, he'd throw a parade. He wasn't sure how to work around to the topic of princesses and runaway girls.

"Are you a football fan?" Angie asked.

"Not really, but I went to every single game in high school."

"Cool," Angie said. "Were you a cheerleader?"

"Nothing like that. I played flute in the marching band."

"Were you ever a prom queen? Or one of the princesses?"

"No way."

Julian noticed a difference in her. When she tossed her head and her brown hair bounced, he guessed that she was using a new shampoo or something. And she was wearing eye makeup. "Did you want to be a princess?"

"That's a childish fantasy. Not something I encourage or condone." She returned to studying her computer check-in. "Should I notify you when these gentlemen check in?"

He nodded. Earlier, when he'd made the reservations, he'd told her that the two agents were relatives, and he wanted to show them a good time. Not much of a cover story, but it was enough to assuage curiosity for a day.

As he and Angie strolled away from the front desk, he looked down at her. "Nice job in directing the conversation."

"I've got a couple of tricks I can teach you. Normal people like Tamara might feel threatened if directly confronted. But if you ask a few pointed questions—

stuff about family or high school or where they grew up—they'll be happy to talk about themselves. Tamara is not our princess."

He held open the front door to Nick's Burlesque. "Maybe we'll find her in here. We're not open for another half hour, but a lot of the performers get here early."

As it turned out, nobody but the bartender was in the performance area, and he was busy prepping the booze, mixers and garnishes. Julian licked his lips. At one time, his favorite stress reliever had been whiskey. With the house lights on, the metallic wallpaper seemed tawdry. The three-foot-tall stage and runway looked plain and dull, except for the three shiny silver poles placed strategically so most of the audience had a view.

Angie hopped onto the runway, grasped one of the poles, braced her other hand on her hip and strutted in a circle around it. "Did I ever tell you that I was a stripper?"

"You might have mentioned it." His gaze riveted to her slender form as she held the pole and leaned backward until the tip of her ponytail touched the runway. Adrenaline gushed through his veins. His heart beat hard and fast.

She glided her hands down her body, and then she raised them quickly, tearing the black-and-white poncho over her head. She removed her platform shoes carefully so she wouldn't accidentally fire the weapon hidden inside. Waving to the bartender, she called out, "Gimme some background music."

"You got it, Angie." He touched a couple of buttons

near the front of the bar, and the space was filled with a throbbing drumbeat.

"I've come down here once or twice to work out. It's great exercise." She hooked her leg around the pole. "Watch this."

He couldn't have looked away if he'd wanted to.

Chapter Twenty

Julian was no stranger to strip clubs and burlesque. Right here at Nick's, he'd watched and auditioned acts that ranged from a magician with disappearing clothes to a contortionist whose joints twisted like a strangely seductive pretzel. Some of these women had magnificent bodies, but none turned him on the way Angie did. Completely covered in a sleeveless black turtleneck tucked into black skinny jeans, she was sexier than a nude chorus line of high-kicking dancers.

He was her audience, and she focused her dark-eyed gaze on him. The rest of the world faded away. Matching the tempo of the heavy drumbeat, she reached high on the pole and pulled herself up with her well-toned arms while her legs coiled and flexed. She slithered higher, swung in a loop and went upside down with her legs spread.

From behind his shoulder, he heard catcalls from other performers who had responded to the beating of the drum. They applauded Angie as she slid to the floor in a split. She climbed again and supported herself in a plank position. No doubt this was good exercise, but the only workout he was considering involved the two of them, naked in his bed.

She wrapped up her pole dance with a front flip, opened her arms to welcome applause and made a sarcastic curtsy. Gathering her poncho and shoes, she jumped down from the stage. "Once you learn these moves, you never forget."

Lola—the performer with the operatic voice—clarified her statement. "Most people have the muscle memory but haven't kept up the strength."

"Better exercise than a spin class." Angie called out a thank-you to the bartender and turned to the four performers. Dressed in street clothes, they could have passed as soccer moms with attitude. "We wanted to talk to you ladies, and I think Jane's dressing room is comfortable."

Julian knew she was taking them to a place where there were no cameras and no microphones. He was content to follow along. After watching her pole dance, it was going to take a while for him to regain his composure.

Lola closed the door and took charge. In spite of her angelic voice, she was a hard-edged leader. "What's the deal, Julian? Something's going on, and we need to know what it is."

An agile gymnastic dancer started a series of stretches and asked, "I don't get it, Lola. Why do you think there's a problem?"

"Take a look around," Lola said. "Julian doesn't usually come down here for a pep talk. Jane and Cara are still staying on the concierge level, being protected.

And I saw a bad guy in the audience—someone I used to know when I worked in Denver."

"Who's that?" Julian asked.

"He calls himself El Jefe, and he belongs to the Fifteen gang. He's deep into the sex trade. While I was onstage, he blew a kiss." She shuddered. "Guys like him make me sick."

"I'll check the tapes," Julian promised. Weeks ago, he'd sent surveillance tapes of El Jefe having dinner with Lorenzo.

"You'll know him right away. He's got the MMXV tattoo on the back of his right hand," Lola added.

"Lola's right," Angie said. "We've got a problem, and we need your help. We're trying to find a runaway girl who is in danger."

He was surprised that she'd chosen to tell the straightforward truth. He watched the four women for their reactions. Lola hardly ever betrayed emotion. The gymnast was more childlike and open. The ballad singer teared up, which didn't mean anything because she wept over every little thing. In his opinion, the most likely princess was Felicity the belly dancer, who had two kids of her own.

Julian directed his comments to her. "Felicity, you might have noticed this girl. She's eight or nine, has brown hair and likes to draw."

"Why do you think I'd notice?"

"The girl said she was helped by a princess. That's why I thought of you."

She preened. "Do you think I look like a princess?"

"Sure," he said. "And you have other kids, so you'd be sympathetic."

"Not to a runaway," Felicity said. "If I caught a kid running away from home, I'd turn her around and take her back where she belongs."

Angie added, "The girl's name is Gigi."

Nothing but blank looks from the four women. Not a princess among them. After telling them to call if they saw Gigi or if El Jefe appeared again, he escorted Angie from the Burlesque. In addition to debugging the rooms for Shanahan and Hemming, he needed to run through surveillance and make identifications on any other members of the Fifteen. He was running out of time.

As they strolled across the three-story lobby on the way to the elevators, Angie tilted her head up and spoke quietly so none of the mics could pick up her words. "There has to be a reason why El Jefe is hanging around."

"To coordinate the start of the operation." The Fifteen must be more involved than the cartel that Damien worked for. He thought of the shoot-out in the bakery. Infighting among powerful criminal gangs was a problem.

His private office was one of the safe places at Nick's. In this space, no one could listen in or watch them. He paced while he talked.

"We need more intel. Obviously, we can't strike up a conversation with El Jefe or any of his minions. Zapata probably has the most detailed information, but he's not likely to let anything slip."

"Especially not to me," she said. "Being at Valentino's when Damien was killed must have put me on his enemies' list."

"I've never gotten a warm, fuzzy vibe from Zapata." The only person who was close enough to Julian and might share information was Lorenzo. "I'll put in a call to Nick."

"Are you sure that's necessary?"

"We need to find out if the timing has changed. Tonight, a combined task force from the FBI and CBI will swoop down and pick up the major players. They'll be caught red-handed and charged. If the schedule is different, the traffickers will get off scot-free."

She stepped in front of him, halting his aimless route. "I hate that you're going to talk to Lorenzo, but I get it."

"I need to have my video guy, Gordon, debug the rooms for Shanahan and Hemming. I hate to leave this in his hands, but I don't have time to do it myself. I've got to trust him while I look at surveillance tapes."

"And I'll leave you to it." She gave him a light kiss on the cheek. "Call me if anything turns up."

AFTER AN HOUR staring at tapes and trying to track the movements of El Jefe, Julian was relieved to have a phone call from Waylon asking him to come out to the barn. "I got something here y'all might want to see."

"Okay." He turned away from the screens. "Did you get the order to leave the barn with three new guys later?"

"You betcha I did. The Baker himself told me."

"I'll be there in a minute."

Before he escaped the dimly lit room full of surveillance screens, Gordon stepped inside. "I have those rooms debugged and clean."

"Did either of my uncles check in yet."

"Not that I know of." Gordon dropped the extra key cards on the desk beside Julian. "Is there anything else you want to talk about?"

"After tonight, it'll all be clear."

If they survived the bust tonight. Hemming told Angie he'd be here at two, and it was already twelve minutes past the hour. He put through an encrypted call to Shanahan, who answered abruptly.

"Julian, I just checked in at the desk. We'll talk later."

"Yes, sir."

Another call came through from Tamara informing him of his uncles' arrival.

The person Julian hadn't heard from was Nick Lorenzo, who he'd called twice. He didn't like the way this was going down.

As he approached the barn, Waylon sauntered out to meet him. This area outside the barn wasn't bugged and didn't have camera surveillance, which meant it was one of the more secure places at Nick's. Julian asked, "What's up?"

"Yesterday I figured out that the real reason for Angie's riding lesson was to search for that little girl. Am I right?"

"How did you know about the girl?"

"I hear things now and then. Could be that little Cara told me." He shrugged. "I think that's it. Cara said something about her imaginary friend. I didn't know it was so important to find her."

Julian was irritated, mad at himself for not trusting the old cowboy with these secrets and hiding the truth from Waylon. "Do you know where she is?"

"No, sir, I sure don't. But I did. A couple of days ago, I could have taken you to her and introduced you. Not that the girl ever told me her name." He took off his hat and pushed his hair back from the accordion-pleated wrinkles on his forehead. "I'm real doggoned sorry I didn't speak up. Wasn't trying to trick you. Nothing like that."

"I believe you." Waylon's motives were innocent enough. He didn't want the little girl to get in trouble. "Tell me what happened."

"This here kid was hanging out in the barn. She'd dragged a blanket and pillow from the bunkhouse and made herself comfy in one of the horse stalls."

"That matches the story Cara told me."

"This little girl feeds me a sob story about how she got stuck here and her mama was coming to pick her up real soon. The mama, she said, was a princess."

Julian winced. Little Gigi wove a complicated web. "You let her stay."

"I didn't see the harm. Next morning when I checked in, she was gone. And she'd done a fine job of tidying up after herself. Heck, I wouldn't know she'd been here, except she left these drawings behind."

He handed over a few sheets of notepaper. The sketches weren't bad for a nine-year-old. Julian could tell that one was supposed to be Cara. Another was a standard version of a princess in a ball gown. There were also sketches of a horse, a dog and a barn. Each was signed in the right corner with a double initial: G. G.

"There's more writing on the back," Waylon said.

Julian turned over the sheets. The Cara sketch was labeled with her name. The dog was Pookie. And the princess was Marigold. "I'll be damned," Julian muttered.

He took out his phone to call Angie, but before she answered, he disconnected. Two of Valentino's dark blue vans raced toward the barn. He and Waylon jumped out of the way just in time. The door on the driver's side was flung open. Zapata lurched out.

Chapter Twenty-One

Frustrated that there wasn't more she could do, Angie flopped into one of the chairs at the table in Jane's suite on the concierge level. Jane placed a steaming mug of coffee in front of her and said, "You might as well relax. Fidgeting won't make the time go faster."

"I'm worried that Julian is going to get into trouble."

"It's like that when you're falling in love. Worry doesn't change anything. Trust and it will turn out fine."

"I hope so."

Though a change in schedule seemed unlikely, Angie feared a surprise switch. The trafficking operation would go into action before they were ready, and the witnesses would disappear. Julian's years of undercover intelligence gathering would be wasted as well as her own efforts. Lorenzo would—once again—evade criminal charges and continue living a charmed life in his Glass Palace.

She'd talked to Marigold and told her to come over here. Maybe she was asking her friend to jump from the frying pan into the fire, but if Marigold was at her side, Angie could protect her. As she raised the mug to her lips, she heard her ringtone. The caller ID showed that Julian was calling, but he hung up before she could answer. Not a good sign. "I wonder what that was about."

"You don't have to explain anything to me," Jane said, "but I'm guessing that you and Julian have something going on."

"You could say that. He's my boyfriend."

"And something more." Jane cocked her head to one side. "I think you two are partners. Are you a cop?"

It was the second time she'd been asked that question in as many days. She must be losing her touch at maintaining an undercover identity. Since Marigold already suspected that Angie was in law enforcement, there didn't seem to be much point in further denial. Still, she put her index finger across her lips and pointed to Cara who was sprawled on the bed with a coloring book. "Let's talk about something else."

"Tell me all about you and Julian. I've never seen him with a girlfriend."

"We hit it off."

"When you're done with your work at Nick's, are you going to leave him with a broken heart?"

"That's not my intention." *What about me? What about my heart?*

"I hate to see him get hurt. He's a good man."

Cara had been coloring the same square of blue for the past several minutes. Clearly, she was listening to the grown-up conversation. Angie said, "It's complicated."

"How so?"

"My work can take me all over the country. Julian is

based in Colorado, and this is where he's going to stay. If we make a commitment, one of us will have to leave our career, and I'm pretty sure that he'd want me to quit. That doesn't work for me. I'm not ready to settle down."

Jane nodded slowly. "Have you talked to him about this?"

"There's no need to talk or discuss. I'm sure he's thinking the same thing I am." Even more frustrated, she bounced to her feet, unable to sit quietly and allow fate to take its course. "We're very much alike, Julian and I. It's like we think with the same brain."

She heard the unmistakable snap of gunfire and ran to the window that gave a view of the barn. Cara had gotten there first and was staring. She saw the vans from Valentino's and armed men ducking for cover. They were under attack, and she was certain that Julian was in the middle of the assault.

She ran into the fourth floor lobby where Muscleman Matt sat at the concierge desk. "Go," she snapped at him. "Julian is in trouble by the barn."

"I'm on it. I'll get the others."

Her phone rang. The call was coming from Julian.

She answered in a flash. "What's going on?"

"A disagreement between Zapata and El Jefe."

"I sent Matt and the other concierge troops to the barn."

"Shanahan is here. He has more agents on the way. We can handle this."

She heard another blast of gunfire. "It definitely doesn't sound like you've got things under control."

"I talked to Lorenzo. He's looking for Marigold, and he doesn't sound happy. You need to warn her."

"Got it."

"There's something else I have to tell you. I wanted to do it in person. But this is what it is." More gunfire. "I love you, Angie." He cleared his throat. "Is there something you want to say to me?"

"You're nuts."

Chapter Twenty-Two

Julian disconnected the call and stared at the screen on his phone. That had to be the worst declaration of love in history! What kind of fool said something like that while dodging bullets? If he survived this, Angie was going to kill him.

He ducked behind the barn door and scooped up a semiautomatic rifle from a man who sprawled bloody and motionless against the side of the bakery van parked inside the barn.

Julian stepped out and sprayed a volley of bullets toward El Jefe, a man he'd never met. He gestured to Waylon. "Open the side door on the van. There are people in there. Get them to safety. Back in the horse stalls."

In spite of the limp, Waylon moved quickly. For an old guy, he got around well. He yanked open the van door and pointed the way to the stalls at the rear of the horse barn.

Two scrawny teenage boys came first, then four young ladies, then a kid. Waylon stepped back, gaping at the open door as Valentino came through. The Baker clenched his forearm around the throat of a pretty young girl whose eyes were as wide as saucers.

"Let her go," Julian growled.

"Then you'll shoot me."

"I don't want to hurt you, but if you don't release the hostage, I'll put a bullet in your brain."

The Baker craned to see around the van. The shooting escalated, and there were two explosions. Grenades? Valentino let go of the child. "Who the hell are those guys? A SWAT team?"

"CBI agents," Julian said with some satisfaction. He caught a glimpse of Hemming in his bulletproof FBI vest. "And the feds."

The Baker's eyebrows raised in disbelief. "You're a cop."

"Yeah."

His team was winning. He could only hope there had been no casualties.

ANGIE PUT THROUGH a call to Marigold, who answered on the first ring. "Almost there," she said. "Coming up the stairs to the fourth floor."

Angie braced herself in front of the door with the Exit sign above it. Marigold burst through. Following her was a girl with straggly brown hair. Marigold pulled the child in front of her, resting her hands upon skinny shoulders. Their eyes were the same tapered shape and greenish-gray color. Their button noses matched.

"This is my daughter," Marigold said. "Georgia Grant."

Two *g*'s equaled Gigi.

Cara—who had obviously been eavesdropping—dashed from her room and flung her arms around her mysterious friend. Both girls chattered like chipmunks as they scampered across the lobby and into the suite.

Angie remembered the call from Julian. "Lorenzo is after you."

"I know." She glanced over her shoulder as if she expected him to appear. "I'm hoping he won't look for me here. There's supposed to be something big going down."

Angie had about a million questions, but her number one priority was to keep them all safe. She poked her head into Jane's suite. "You have two minutes to grab everything you need. We're going to Julian's room on the seventh floor."

"Good plan," Marigold said. "I helped design this building, and Julian's suite is the safest place to be."

While Jane and the two kids gathered up their things, she turned to her friend. "Give me a brief explanation."

"When I was a teenager and Nick Lorenzo took an interest in me, I fell in love. He gave me expensive jewelry and clothes and cash. Just about the time he started to lose interest, I found out I was pregnant."

In her head, Angie did the math. It had been eleven years since she'd seen Marigold, and Gigi was nine years old according to Cara. "Go on."

"He shipped me off to live with a cousin in the mountains while I was pregnant. After the baby was born, we got back together, but he didn't want anything to do with Gigi. He arranged for her to be taken care of by a family in a small mountain town."

"Why didn't you go to the police?"

"Biding my time," she said. "He had enough to put me in jail, and he used Gigi's safety to control me. I was convinced that there was nothing I could do. I'd never be free. But then, I started collecting evidence on him."

"What kind of evidence."

"Documents, recorded conversations, photos. Trust me, there's a ton of proof. I can take down Nick, Zapata and most of his top guys." She dashed away an angry tear. "He wants me dead. And Gigi, too."

"That's not going to happen."

If they escaped in one piece, Hemming and Shanahan would be thrilled. Angie herded Marigold, Jane, Cara and Gigi into the enclosed stairwell and up to the seventh floor. The entire floor was devoted to only two luxury suites. The foyer was often used for receptions and cocktail parties. It was a huge space with a high glass ceiling in an A-frame design like the one on the first floor. Angie opened the door to Julian's suite using the code he'd given her.

She called his phone, expecting to leave a message. Instead, he answered.

"We're safe," she said. "In your suite."

"Stay where you are. I'm coming. We have Zapata and Valentino in custody, but Lorenzo just arrived in front. He went into the lobby."

She glanced at the door to the suite. At Valentino's bakery she'd seen the type of firepower these guys used. They could blast through the door. She took the Glock and two clips from the secret compartment in Julian's bedroom. As she stalked through the front room, she snapped out an order. "Stay here. Help is on the way."

"Where are you going?" Jane asked.

"I'm going to stall these creeps."

In the foyer, she took a position in front of the elevator. The digital numbers showed that the elevator was stopped on the fourth floor. No doubt, when Lorenzo was done searching there, he'd come up here. And she'd be ready. Her Glock was no match for his weapons, but she was smarter and more determined. For eleven years, she'd hated this guy. When she'd heard how he tortured Marigold and Gigi, Angie's loathing doubled. She wouldn't hesitate to shoot him.

The numbers on the elevator showed it ascending to the fifth floor, the sixth and here. When the doors whooshed open, she had the drop on Lorenzo and two henchmen, including Rudy.

"Get out," she said. "Don't get clever or I'll shoot."

Lorenzo gestured to the men standing behind him. "Do as she says. Angie is a reasonable woman. I'm sure we can come to an agreement."

Her gun didn't waver in her two-handed grip as she stared at this unspeakably dangerous predator. Shooting him would be a favor to humanity. "Drop your weapons."

Rudy and the other guy exchanged a smirk, but Lorenzo's face was blank. When he talked, his lips barely moved. His voice was pitched at a low baritone that was probably supposed to convince her that she had nothing to worry about. To Angie, he sounded like the warning castanets of a rattlesnake about to strike.

"I'm not going to hurt Marigold," he said. "I'm trying to do the right thing for her and for Gigi."

"Why should I believe you?"

"If I could, I'd let you talk to her social worker. Gigi is a runaway, a naughty little girl."

That was exactly what the authority figures said about her when she was a foster child desperate for understanding. "Your gun. On the floor. Now."

"You haven't got a chance. There are three of us and only one of you."

"If any of you—and that includes you, Rudy—make a move toward me, I'll start firing. I'm pretty sure that I can't get all of you, so I'll concentrate on one target. You, Lorenzo. Before your boys take me down, I can get three bullets into you."

He studied her for a moment with his cold, dark eyes. "I don't believe you. I don't think you're a killer."

Behind her back, she heard a door open and slam shut. Calamity Jane strode forward with her whip in hand. She wore the belt she used in her stage act—three throwing knives on each side. "What about me? Am I a killer?"

"This isn't your fight, Jane."

"You abused a child. I can't let that pass."

"Don't be a bitch." He stuck out his hand. "Give me the damn whip."

"You asked for it." She snapped the whip at his gun hand and disarmed him. His weapon clattered to the floor. "Now, you other two boys."

The whip flicked restlessly across the floor like a hungry serpent. The guy Angie didn't recognize set his weapon down and stepped back, but Rudy made a stand. He lifted his semiautomatic gun and prepared to shoot. Angie fired first. She wasn't a skilled markswoman and she wasn't familiar with Julian's Glock, but she managed to hit Rudy's gun and throw off his aim. A spray of bullets peppered the carpet near her feet. She felt a sharp sting in her lower leg and went down. She'd been shot.

Jane attacked with her whip, pinning Rudy's arms to his side. When she switched to her throwing knives, Lorenzo raised his hands over his head.

The other guy tried to flee, and Jane used her knife. It only took one hit in the wall in front of him to convince him to stop running and drop to his knees.

They'd won.

The second elevator arrived on the seventh floor. Julian and Muscleman emerged. If they were surprised, they didn't show it. Muscleman used zip ties to secure their prisoners.

Julian knelt beside her on the floor. He cradled her against his chest and gazed into her eyes. "Is there something you want to tell me?"

"For your information, the L-word doesn't count when bullets are flying, and you think you might be killed. And what's the point? No matter how we feel about each other, I'm not going to quit my job and stay in Colorado."

"I didn't ask you to do that." He pulled her closer. "Come on, Angie. Say it."

"Are you aware that I'm bleeding?"

"Who shot you? Was it Lorenzo?"

"Rudy."

"As if I needed another excuse to kill that traitor?"

She patted his cheek. "Maybe I do love you, after all."

Epilogue

The grand reopening of Nick's, which was now called The Double L—which stood for *Lucky Leif's*—was scheduled for December first, and it was the first time Angie had been back in Colorado since the joint FBI and CBI bust of Lorenzo's human trafficking network. Though their procedure had been thrown off by the change in timing, the final takedown was perfection with zero casualties and—thanks to perfect bookkeeping from Marigold—tons of evidence in the USA, Colombia and Mexico.

She'd spoken to Julian on the phone, talking for hours, but had only seen him twice.

Marigold had picked her up at the airport and was driving to the grand reopening. She zipped along the mountain roads, talking a mile a minute. "Are you sure you're okay? I love the cane, by the way."

"I don't really need the walking stick anymore. Wearing a cast was awful, but I'm a hundred percent fine."

"That's what Julian is going to say," she teased.

Angie didn't want to talk about herself. She was

hyped to see her friends. "Tell me about the girls, Gigi and Cara?"

"Doing great. And we have a day care for the other kids of employees. The Double L is more family-oriented. Leif got rid of the casino but kept sports betting and OTB. The Burlesque is a lounge with no nudity and lots of variety acts."

"I heard that Calamity Jane runs the place."

"She does that and special events. I do the decor and decorations."

"And Leif and Tamara are co-owners."

Soon they'd be married, which was wonderful. While they continued to chat, she couldn't stop thinking about Julian. He'd come to see her once in the hospital in DC. and one other time to make sure she got home and had everything she needed.

She still hadn't told him that she loved him.

Of course, she did. But she hadn't said the words.

A light dusting of snow covered the meadow leading to The Double L. Pretty as a postcard with hundreds of Christmas lights. At the entrance, valets in Santa hats took Marigold's car. Julian stood waiting at the top of the stairs.

When she stepped into his embrace, he lifted her off the ground and twirled her around. She wanted to tell him right now. The L-word was at the tip of her tongue.

Before she could speak, he said, "I have a surprise for you. I quit."

Was she supposed to be happy about this? "I don't understand."

"I like working undercover, but my career for the

CBI is pretty much over. Half the criminals in the state know who I am and what I look like. But I can start over if I join the FBI."

"But you don't have the training."

"I took some special qualifying courses in Quantico. That's what I've been doing for the past six weeks when I wanted to be hovering at your bedside. I was learning to be a field agent."

"We can work together," she said. "We'll be partners."

"That's the plan."

She snuggled against his chest. "I love you with a capital *L*."

"And that, my darling, is no lie."

* * * * *

COMING NEXT MONTH FROM

HARLEQUIN

INTRIGUE

#2037 TARGETING THE DEPUTY
Mercy Ridge Lawmen • by Delores Fossen

After narrowly escaping an attempt on his life, Deputy Leo Logan is shocked to learn the reason for the attack is his custody battle for his son with his ex, Olivia Nash. To catch the real killer, he'll have to keep them both close—and risk falling for Olivia all over again.

#2038 CONARD COUNTY: CHRISTMAS BODYGUARD
Conard County: The Next Generation • by Rachel Lee

Security expert Hale Scribner doesn't get personal with clients. Ever. But having evidence that could put away a notoriously shady CEO doesn't make Allie Burton his standard low-risk charge. With an assassin trailing them 24/7, they'll need a Christmas miracle to survive the danger...and their undeniable attraction.

#2039 TEXAS ABDUCTION
An O'Connor Family Mystery • by Barb Han

When Cheyenne O'Connor's friend goes missing, she partners with her estranged husband, rancher Riggs O'Connor, for answers. During their investigation, evidence emerges suggesting their daughter—who everyone claims died at childbirth—might be alive and somehow connected. Riggs and Cheyenne are determined to find out what really happened...and if their little girl will be coming home after all.

#2040 MOUNTAINSIDE MURDER
A North Star Novel Series • by Nicole Helm

North Star undercover operative Sabrina Killian is on a hit man's trail and doesn't want help from Wyoming search and rescue ranger Connor Lindstrom. But the persistent ex-SEAL is the killer's real target. Will Sabrina and Connor's most dangerous secrets even the odds—or take them out for good?

#2041 ALASKAN CHRISTMAS ESCAPE
Fugitive Heroes: Topaz Unit • by Juno Rushdan

With an elite CIA kill squad locating hacker Zenobia Hanley's Alaska wilderness hideout, it's up to her mysterious SEAL neighbor, John Lowry, to save her from capture. Regardless of the risks and secrets they're both hiding, John's determined to protect Zee because there's more at stake this Christmas than just their lives...

#2042 BAYOU CHRISTMAS DISAPPEARANCE
by Denise N. Wheatley

Mona Avery is determined to investigate a high-profile missing person case in the Louisiana bayou before heading home for Christmas. Stubborn detective Dillon Reed insists she's more of a hindrance than a help. But when a killer wants Mona's story silenced, only Dillon can keep her safe...

HICNM1121

SPECIAL EXCERPT FROM

HARLEQUIN

INTRIGUE

When she discovers high-level corruption at her job, accountant Allie Burton finds herself—reluctantly—in desperate need of a bodyguard. Tall, ruggedly handsome and terse, Hale Scribner goes all in to save lives, even if it means staying on the move, going from town to town. But once they hit the bucolic Conard County, Allie puts her foot down and demands a traditional Christmas celebration... which may be how they lure a killer to his prey...

Keep reading for a sneak peek at Conard County: Christmas Bodyguard, *part of Conard County: The Next Generation, from* New York Times *bestselling author Rachel Lee.*

"You need a bodyguard."

Allie Burton's jaw dropped as soon as her dad's old friend Detective Max Roles spoke the words.

It took a few beats for Allie to reply. "Oh, come on, Max. That's over-the-top. I'm sure Mr. Ellis was talking about all his international businesses, about protecting his companies. He said he'd put the auditing firm on it."

Max was getting up in years. His jowls made him look like a bloodhound with a bald head. Allie had known him all her life, thanks to his friendship with her father, who had died years ago. She trusted him, but this?

"What were his *exact* words, Allie?"

She pulled them up from recent memory. "He said, *exactly*, that I shouldn't tell anyone anything about what I'd found in the books."

Max shook his head. "And the rest?"

She shrugged. "He said, and I quote, *Bad things can happen*. Well, of course they could. He's a tycoon with companies all over the world. Any irregularity in the books could cause big problems."

"Right," Max said. "I want you to think about that. Bad things can happen."

Allie frowned. "I guess you're one of the people I shouldn't have told about this. I thought you'd laugh and wouldn't tell anyone."

HIEXP1121

"I won't tell anyone except the bodyguard you're going to hire. You've been on the inside of Jasper Ellis's success."

"So what?"

Max leaned forward. "I have nothing against the man's success. We've been investigating him for years, and we've never found a thing we could hang on him. He's good at covering evidence."

"You've been investigating him for what?"

Max blew a cloud. "For the unexplained disappearances and supposed suicides of a number of his employees."

Allie felt a chill run down her spine. Her own dismissal of the situation began to feel naive. "You're kidding," she murmured.

"I wish I was. Here's the thing. At first it could be dismissed. But then the numbers really caught our attention and we started looking into it. Nothing traces directly back to Ellis except he's at the top of the pyramid. You may remember I fought against you going to work for him."

Allie did. Max had strenuously argued with her, something he never did. He was not a man given to conspiracy theories. A hard-nosed detective, he stuck to the facts. He seemed to have some facts right now.

"So I'm going to call that bodyguard. I've known him for years, since he was still in the Marines. I trust him with your life. And you're not leaving my house before he gets here."

"God, Max!"

"Just go make yourself a cup of whatever. But you are *not* going anywhere."

He punctuated those words like bullet shots. Truly shaken, Allie rose to get that drink. She trusted Max. Completely. He'd been like an uncle to her for most of her life. If Max said it, it was true.

As she passed through the short hallway, she saw her reflection in the full-length mirror. Allie paused, wondering who that woman in there was. She felt so changed that she shouldn't look the same. Neat dark blue business slack suit, a blue-striped button-down shirt, collar open. Her ash-blond hair in a fluffed, loose short cut because she didn't feel like fussing with it. A trim every couple of weeks solved that problem.

A bodyguard? The thought sent a tendril of ice creeping along her spine. Seriously?

HIEXP1121